Fight at Felicidad

Thora Dowling is on her way to join her fiancé, Marshal Ralph Kirkpatrick, in Felicidad. Whilst waiting for the stagecoach, she witnesses the murder of three men and is rescued by the arrival of Elias Pitt, a gambler also heading for the town.

Kirkpatrick identifies the killer as Old Man Hennessey, leader of the feared Hennessey family. Together with Pitt, he arrests the man and holds him for trial. But will Hennessey remain in jail for long with his family determined to rescue him whatever the cost?

Danger faces Kirkpatrick, Pitt and Thora every step towards the final, bloody showdown. Can justice be done?

Fight at Felicidad

Steven Gray

A Black Horse Western

ROBERT HALE · LONDON

© Steven Gray 2005
First published in Great Britain 2005

ISBN 0 7090 7794 7

Robert Hale Limited
Clerkenwell House
Clerkenwell Green
London EC1R 0HT

Typeset by
Derek Doyle & Associates, Shaw Heath.
Printed and bound in Great Britain by
Antony Rowe Limited, Wiltshire

CHAPTER ONE

Old Man Hennessey strode through Felicidad in a toweringly foul mood.

Much to everyone's relief he'd been on his way to the livery stable and was going home without anyone being hurt, when Jake Carney sidled up to him and whispered that Adam Mills was making up to Hennessey's girl down at Carney's saloon. That alone would have been enough to send Hennessey into a rage but bad blood already existed between him and Mills, mostly because Mills had once worked out at Hennessey's ranch and knew all about the rustling that went on there.

Hennessey immediately turned round to stalk back to the redlight district. Wisely everyone – cowboys, ranch-owners, townsfolk, even the law – kept well out of his way. Hennessey was unpredictable at the best of times. Now with a face as black as thunder, thick hands hovering above his Colt .45 on one hip and his Bowie knife on the other, who knew what he might do?

Trouble was coming to Carney's saloon over one of

the girls who worked there, as trouble often did.

Carney's stood all alone at the far end of Felicidad's small but thriving redlight district. It gave the area a bad name being little more than a mud hut where Carney sold watered down beer and rotgut whiskey, while anyone stupid enough to get into a card game there was asking to be cheated out of all his money.

Knowing who was on his way and why, several of the more prudent customers got out quick while the rest stayed to gawp.

Hennessey reached the saloon and slammed the door back so hard the whole building shuddered. He stepped inside.

'Mills!' he roared.

Everything and everyone came to a halt.

Mills was over by the far wall with the girl, Lizzie. Caught up in talking to one another, believing Old Man Hennessey had left town, they were about the only two in the place who hadn't known danger was approaching. Now they both swung round, shocked at being caught.

'Get away from her, you sonofabitch!'

Most times Mills would have done what he was told, would have said he and Lizzie were just talking, that he meant no harm. He'd probably run away, for which no one would have blamed him, leaving Lizzie on her own to take all the blame. But he'd been drinking and was drunk. If he'd been sober he wouldn't have been talking to Lizzie in the first place. And when he was drunk he had a quick temper. So he stood his ground.

'You, I'll deal with later,' Hennessey shouted, pointing a finger at the white-faced and trembling Lizzie.

'I didn't . . .' the girl began.

She got no further before Hennessey was by her side. He shoved her out of the way so hard that she fell to the floor. Then he turned his attention on Mills.

One of Carney's customers pulled Lizzie to her feet. She quickly escaped the room, not wanting to be anywhere near Hennessey when he won the fight, knowing he would then come to punish her for just doing her job. The rest of the men in the place stood up, crowding around the two antagonists, shouting out their encouragement and excitement.

With a yell Hennessey charged Mills. Hennessey was a bully and a dirty fighter. But he was also predictable. He just punched and kicked, using his strength to put his opponent on the ground as quickly as possible.

Mills had seen Hennessey fight many a time and was ready. He ducked the first blow and slammed a fist into Hennessey's stomach. The man staggered a little but at once came on to Mills again. Mills took the second blow on the side of his face, grunting with pain, almost falling, but somehow he managed to block the next one. Before Hennessey could hit him again, he flung himself at the man, grappling him, grimacing as he was kicked hard on the shin.

They both tumbled to the floor, knocking over a table. Drink flew everywhere and glasses smashed, causing the onlookers to jump out of the way.

Hennessey heaved up, throwing Mills off him but even as he was getting to his feet, Mills hit him again.

The blow wasn't that hard but it caught Hennessey off-balance. He fell awkwardly, striking his head on the table-leg. He wasn't knocked out but the impact made him groggy.

Mills seized his chance. He grabbed hold of Hennessey's hair and banged the man's head down once, twice, on the floor as hard as he could. Hennessey's eyes glazed over and he went limp. Mills was the victor.

He stood up, breathing heavily, sucking his bloody knuckles, looking down on the unconscious Hennessey. His moment of triumph didn't last long.

Christ, what had he done? He sobered quickly as he realized exactly what it was he had done! He'd thrashed Old Man Hennessey in front of witnesses. The man would never forgive him. Better that he should have let Hennessey beat him up. The matter might then have been forgotten, at least as far as Mills was concerned. Now, once the Old Man recovered, Mills's life wouldn't amount to a hill of beans. Hennessey would be out for revenge.

'Hell, Adam,' Carney said, after pushing through the suddenly silent crowd and staring down at Hennessey's prone body. 'Now look what you've gone and done. He ain't gonna like this.'

An understatement if ever there was one.

'Nor is the rest of the clan,' Carney went on.

While the saloon-owner wasn't sorry at seeing Hennessey get a taste of his own medicine, he was sorry it had happened in his saloon. He'd known it would come to a fight when he told Hennessey about Mills and Lizzie but he'd been sure Hennessey would win the fight. He always did. Now he'd lost! Carney would have to find some way to make up to Hennessey for what had happened, make sure the blame for it all lay with Lizzie. He thought it would be best for everyone if Mills made himself scarce.

'You'd better get the hell out of here.'

Good advice.

Mills took it. He decided that not only would he leave Carney's he'd also leave Felicidad.

Pronto.

By the time Marshal Kirkpatrick, accompanied by his deputy, Dave Vaughan, arrived at Carney's he was too late. It was quiet and nearly everyone had gone home, not wanting Hennessey to know they'd watched his downfall. And those few hardcases left would never admit to having seen or heard a thing. To his surprise, a dazed Hennessey sat in the corner, looking bruised and bloody, holding a piece of rag to his mouth. He was muttering something about revenge. From somewhere out the back Kirkpatrick could hear a woman crying. Angrily, he thought that a woman crying at Carney's was nothing unusual.

'What happened here?' he demanded of Jake Carney.

'It was Lizzie's fault,' Carney said with a glance at the door so that Kirkpatrick knew it was Lizzie who was crying. 'She knew the Old Man was in town but the stupid whore insisted on flirting with Adam Mills. Hennessey came here to sort 'em both out.'

9

'I just wonder how Hennessey found out about them,' Kirkpatrick said, not expecting a reply. 'And Mills did this to Hennessey?'

'Yeah. Knocked him clean out. The damn idiot.'

'I'll get the bastard,' Hennessey mumbled.

Thinking the Old Man didn't look capable of doing anything, Kirkpatrick tried to hide a smile. It wasn't often anyone got the better of Hennessey. He wished he'd been there to witness it.

'Where is Mills now?'

'He ran off.' Carney grinned.

'Has he left Felicidad?'

'Dunno, but if he's got any sense he will've.'

'Keep Hennessey here until the morning. Don't let him ride after Mills.' It was an order but Kirkpatrick had no real belief that Carney would even try to obey him.

With nothing for them to do, Kirkpatrick sent his deputy home while he went down to the livery stable to find out if Mills had left Felicidad and if he hadn't to make sure he did.

'Yeah he rode off,' the stable owner said. 'Woke me up. Just like you. Some people have no consideration.'

Kirkpatrick took no notice of the man's grumbling. 'What time was that?'

' 'Bout midnight. Soon after anyhow.'

'Did he say anything?'

'Not much. Just that he was fleeing from Hennessey and was gonna ride to Freeman's Station and wait there for the morning stage to Lordsburg.'

'Was he drunk?'

'Well he'd've to be to get into it with Hennessey wouldn't he?' the man said with a toothless grin. 'But he weren't drunk enough to be incapable. He should make it to Freeman's all right.'

And hopefully Hennessey would not recover until it was too late for him to do anything except rant and rave for a while. He couldn't chase Mills if he didn't know where the man had gone. And if Mills knew what was good for him he'd never come back to Felicidad.

It was over before it had begun. Kirkpatrick need not do anything.

Instead he could look forward to Thora's arrival. She should be here sometime tomorrow afternoon.

CHAPTER TWO

Elias Pitt halted his horse in the shade of a group of poplar trees before the treeline gave way to a steep hillside of rocks and shale. Up here the air was clear. He could easily make out the stagecoach road that headed in a long, straight line all the way across the reddish-brown valley to the foothills of the Mimbres Mountains.

'Thank God,' he said out loud, perhaps to himself or perhaps to his horse. 'Nearly there.'

All he had to do was follow the road to Freeman's Stage Station and there take the turn-off towards Felicidad.

He gulped warm water from the canteen and taking off his low-crowned hat wiped his face and neck with his bandanna. It was early May and by noon it was already hot. He hoped to make enough money to get in and out of Felicidad before the stifling heat of summer and then head for somewhere in the higher country, like Santa Fe, where it would be cooler. He was only travelling to the town because a friend had told him that easy money could be made playing poker in the saloons there.

Pitt was a gambler. Had been for years. A good one too who didn't cheat because he didn't have to. He lived by his wits and he liked to live well.

He didn't know how he'd come to realize he was a good card-player; shuffling, dealing and winning were things that had always seemed to come naturally. His parents were upset when he said he wasn't going to work on their farm and instead was heading West to seek his fortune, but as he had two younger brothers they didn't try to stop him.

That had been almost seventeen years ago and he was now thirty-three. He was tall and lean with blue eyes, short black hair and a trim handlebar moustache. He looked like a gambler, wearing low-heeled boots, dark trousers and matching vest, a white shirt and a black frockcoat. He'd been back home several times only to find that he and his family no longer had anything in common. He was unhappy about that but it was true and he couldn't change it.

'Come on, girl,' he said and clicked the sturdy mare into a walk. 'It won't be long now.'

And they could both rest up and slake away the thirst of the long journey.

As if she understood the horse pricked up her ears and started to pick a way through the rocks down to the valley floor.

'All being well the stage to Felicidad should be here in fifteen, twenty minutes,' Clint Freeman said.

He didn't sound very hopeful and Thora Dowling sighed. She had already been here since the Wells

13

Fargo stage dropped her off at just gone ten o'clock that morning. And if her experience of travelling in the West was anything to go by she could still be waiting for an hour or more. If the stagecoach arrived at all!

'Would you like another coffee while you wait, miss?'

'Oh no, thank you,' Thora said quickly. Mr Freeman's coffee was lukewarm and exceedingly strong, leaving behind a bitter taste.

She turned from where she was looking out of the window at the country beyond the stage station. How vast New Mexico was, never-ending, empty. How could she come to like it? It was so different to the rolling, gentle country she was used to. Yet it was beautiful too: the dun coloured and dusty desert was brightened by spring flowers of all shades while above the sky was a perfect blue.

And she knew some of her doubts were because she was tired after her long and tedious journey. Everything would be all right once she saw Ralph again. She gave a happy sigh. Once she was Mrs Kirkpatrick. She loved Ralph so much she would settle anywhere with him.

And now, after so many days travel, she was almost at her destination. She had only to catch the connecting coach and ride the last few miles into Felicidad. With luck she should be there by mid-afternoon. What would Felicidad be like? What would her new home, as a wife, be like?

She hoped it wasn't anything like Freeman's stage-coach station which was very small, just an adobe hut

14

with homemade and uncomfortable furniture, and a corral and barn outside. Primitive. And none too clean, a layer of dust covering every surface. The midday meal Freeman had offered her was no better than his coffee. Although she hadn't wanted to upset the man, who was very kind and polite, Thora had left most of the greasy pork and beans. Freeman didn't seem to mind. Maybe he was used to it.

She thought it must be lonely all the way out here, in the middle of nowhere. Freeman was alone except for his horse-handler, a young lad of about sixteen, who was called Jamie and who so far hadn't said a word in her presence.

And today there was just one other passenger. A man waiting for the Wells Fargo stage to Lordsburg. He had a nasty bruise on his face and a cut lip. He'd ridden into the station on a played out horse from the direction of Felicidad soon after Thora had arrived there. He'd been very cross when he found the stagecoach to Nogales had already called at Freeman's and gone on its way. And he was obviously worried over something because he spent the time pacing across the floor and staring out of the window. His eyes looked scared.

Mills was scared.

He knew he'd made a mistake in deciding to wait for the stagecoach. He should have ridden on except that his horse couldn't have gone much further. Terrified that Hennessey would come after him, he'd left Felicidad soon after midnight the previous night. When he realized there was no pursuit he'd holed up to wait for morning. Another mistake. He should have ridden through the night, taken his chances on his horse not having an accident in the dark.

But he'd believed he would reach Freeman's with more than enough time to catch the early stagecoach to Nogales. But, wouldn't you know, for about the first time in its history it had been running early! Now he was stuck here waiting for the stage in the opposite direction to Lordsburg which, of course, was late.

Not that it mattered which way he went so long as he actually went somewhere. For Hennessey might well work out that Mills would head for the Wells Fargo stage and then the railroad, and follow him here in the hope of catching up.

Now he said, 'I'll have some of that coffee, Clint. Hell, where's the stage? It should've been here a coupla hours ago.'

'It's delayed for some reason,' Freeman replied as if that was a regular occurrence and nothing to worry about. 'It'll be here soon. And watch your language in front of a lady. Here.'

With a shaky hand Mills took the mug of coffee Freeman handed him.

'I don't see why I can't hire one of your horses.'

'I already said you can't. We need 'em here for the coaches.' Sounding impatient with the man, Freeman turned from him back to Thora. 'Would you like to freshen up, miss?'

The privy was out back. So far Thora had refused to even think about using it because she was sure it would be smelly and dirty. But now she knew she would never complete the journey in comfort if she didn't pluck up courage to do so.

She nodded.

'There's a towel and soap out there,' Freeman added as he opened the door that led to a short corridor and the rear door to the yard.

Thora picked up her reticule and went outside, making her way across the dusty yard to the privy. It was very hot, with hardly a breath of air; and this was only May! Still Mr Freeman had said it was much cooler near the mountains.

Thankfully the privy wasn't as bad as she imagined, even the towel on which she wiped her hands was reasonably clean. Wanting to look her best for Ralph she took off her bonnet so she could comb her brown hair and secure it into a tidy bun. After that she tried to bang the worst of the dirt from her skirt and jacket.

Feeling better she went back to the house. Her heart felt suddenly light. The stagecoach should be here soon and she could be on her way.

She reached the door to the main room just as the outer door banged back, letting in a shaft of hot sunlight. Perhaps it was the driver ... Something stopped her. Something was wrong.

Everything happened quickly.

Through the partly open door, she was aware of Freeman and Jamie looking up and then glancing apprehensively at one another. The waiting passenger gave a cry of fright and backed away from the newcomer, his hands out before him.

She saw that the man was in his late fifties. He was quite tall and well built, stocky, even. He had stringy greying hair hanging almost to his shoulders and dark eyes that seemed to spark with fury. His left cheek was disfigured by an ugly scar. And he too had bruises on his face.

Thora was instinctively frightened of him and so it appeared were the three men.

'Mills!' he shouted loudly. 'You sonofabitch! Thought you'd get away from me, didn't you? Well, you ain't.'

And to Thora's alarm he drew his gun.

'Hey, we don't want no trouble here,' Freeman said.

At the same time Mills said in a pleading tone, 'Hell, Bernie, I'm sorry. It won't happen again.'

'Sorry!' the man yelled. 'You made me look a fool in front of my pals. You beat me. You gave me these.' With his free hand he indicated his bruises. 'I'll make you goddamned sorry.'

Thora watched wide-eyed. She was aware of her heart pounding so hard she feared it would burst and her mouth was so dry she couldn't swallow.

'No, Bernie, please.'

'Sonofabitch,' the man said and pulled the trigger.

'Christ!' Jamie cried and jumped out of the way.

'Oh!' Thora gave a small squeak of shock as the loud noise made her jump. To her horror she realized Mills had been shot.

Bright red blood appeared on his chest, sprayed around the room and he staggered. He tripped over his feet and collapsed on the floor. And didn't move. He was dead.

Thora couldn't believe it. She had just watched a

man be shot to death! Murdered! She dragged her horrified eyes away from the body. Her stomach churned and she hoped she wasn't going to be sick.

Freeman dived for the back wall where a rifle hung on pegs. He didn't make it.

The man turned towards him. He was smiling now, eyes glinting with excitement and pleasure. 'Can't have no witnesses,' he said. 'Sorry guys.'

And just like that he fired several times, shooting first Jamie and then Freeman. Jamie cried out but Freeman made no sound as he fell. Jamie was still alive but the man shot him again and again, until he too was dead.

Thora's hand went to her mouth to stop herself screaming and she took a hesitant step backwards.

'Please,' she thought, 'don't let him know I'm here. Let him leave. Please.'

But some movement, a slight noise, must have alerted the killer. He swung round in her direction and seemed to stare straight through the door into her terrified eyes. He took a step towards her.

Desperately Thora looked round. She had nowhere to go. Nowhere to hide.

CHAPTER THREE

It was even hotter when Pitt reached the valley and he kept his horse to a gentle walk. He saw no one and nothing until at last the stagecoach station came into view. Even as he sighed with relief he came to a startled halt. He thought he'd heard a shot.

And as he listened there came several more shots, all fired quickly, followed by an ominous silence. Pitt stood up in the stirrups and stared hard towards the buildings. They were too far away for him to make out anything. Was the place under attack? By robbers? Indians perhaps, although he thought that was unlikely these days.

He didn't know anything about Freeman's place but if it was anything like other frontier stage stations it would be run by one man with at most a couple of assistants. There might still be time to help them.

Pitt didn't hesitate. He dug spurs into his horse's sides. She responded and took off at an all-out gallop.

Trembling violently, hardly able to see for the tears in

her eyes, Thora backed slowly away down the corridor. Perhaps she could reach the door to the yard. But then what? There was nowhere outside to hide. Except the privy. That was no use, the man had all the time in the world to search for her and would find her. She was going to be shot and killed. She had no doubt the man would shoot her. He wouldn't want a witness to the fact that he'd murdered three men in cold blood. The fact that she was a young woman would make no difference.

The door was slowly opening!

Thora braced herself, determined not to plead for her life nor to scream.

Even as he must see her, the killer stopped and swore. In the same moment Thora heard what he must have done. The sound of a galloping horse getting ever closer. Rescue! But, oh God, supposing the killer shot whoever was coming here? Somehow she would have to warn the rider. She couldn't just let him ride into danger. Then the man swore again and the outer door opened and closed.

He was gone! Wasn't he? Fearing a trick, Thora didn't dare look to find out. But a few seconds later she heard him ride away. He really had left.

Thora tried to move but found she couldn't. Her legs began to wobble and she sat down on the floor. Tears of fright, of relief, poured down her cheeks.

As he approached the station, Pitt glimpsed another horse being ridden away, fast, raising up a spiral of dust, before disappearing behind a dip of the land. Was he too late? Whatever had happened here,

21

whether it was over or not, he wasn't about to take any chances.

He dismounted at the side of the house, where no windows overlooked the yard, and eased his rifle from its scabbard. Keeping to the wall of the house, he inched his way round to the door, using the rifle barrel to push it open. No one shot at him so he stepped inside out of the sun. His eyes quickly adjusted to the darkness of the room.

'Oh, hell!'

He saw three men, one no more than a boy, shot to death. That they were dead he could tell instantly from all the blood and the way the bodies lay. None of them had managed to draw his gun. In fact one of the men was unarmed and had obviously been making for the rifle on the back wall. Taking in the scene, Pitt's sharp eyes noticed four mugs on the table in one corner. Did that mean the fourth person had been whoever did this and then rode away or was someone else here?

If anyone else was dead or hiding it had to be on the other side of the door opposite. His heart beating loudly, he crossed the room quickly and quietly and opened the door on to a short, dark corridor.

A gasp!

Pitt swung round, raising his rifle.

The gasp turned into a scream, making him jump.

A girl crouched by the wall. She was about twenty-five and somewhat plump with brown hair and brown eyes. She was dressed in travelling clothes. While she might in normal circumstances be quite nice looking at the moment she was white-faced and wide-eyed with terror. She obviously posed no threat.

'I'm sorry,' Pitt said and quickly lowered the rifle. 'I didn't mean to frighten you. It's all right. Whoever shot those men has gone. You're safe now.'

With a cry Thora scrambled up and threw herself against his chest. Between sobs and gasps, she gulped out, 'It was awful. He just shot them. I was so scared. He knew I was here. He was coming for me.'

'It's all right,' Pitt repeated. 'He's ridden away.' He hugged her close until at last she calmed down. Once she had stopped crying he held her at arm's length and said, 'Let's get you some coffee.'

'Not in there. With them.'

'No, stay here.'

'Don't leave me alone.' Thora clawed at his arm.

'I won't be a minute.' Pitt went into the main room and soon returned with a chair on which Thora sank and a mug of coffee.

This time she didn't care what the coffee tasted like. She sipped at it gratefully, having to hold the mug in both hands because she was shaking so hard.

'What happened?' Pitt asked. Taking hold of the mug he hunkered down in front of her.

'This man . . . he came in. He just shot them. I've never seen a dead body before.' Tears threatened again.

'Take your time, Miss. . . ?'

'Thora Dowling.'

'Elias Pitt,' Pitt introduced himself. 'Go on. Tell me about it.'

'I was waiting for the stagecoach to Felicidad, the other passenger wanted the Wells Fargo stage going to Lordsburg. He was very anxious about it. Mr Freeman said both coaches should be here soon. But they're not, are they?'

'No.'

'Then this man burst in and yelled something at the passenger . . .'

'They knew one another?'

'Yes.' Thora nodded.

Pitt thought that made it unlikely this was a robbery gone wrong.

'The newcomer called the passenger Mills. He swore at him and then shot him. There was so much blood. It went everywhere.' She shuddered. 'He said he didn't want any witnesses and shot Mr Freeman and Jamie. It was dreadful. They never stood a chance.' She put her head in her hands and bent forward, willing herself not to faint. Finally she was able to go on. 'He was coming to look for me too but he must have heard you. Anyway he left. Thank God!'

'Had the man, Mills, said anything about why he was anxious or spoken about the killer?'

'Not in my hearing. But he must have been trying to run away from his murderer, mustn't he?'

'Yeah, likely. Did you recognize the killer?'

'Oh no, I'm a stranger here. But,' her eyes took on a resolute gleam, 'I would most certainly recognize him again! Oh and Mills called him Bernie. I remember that! Do you know who that could be?'

'No. I'm a stranger to the area too.'

'Oh! Well, anyway I intend to tell Ralph all about this man and what he did.'

'Ralph?'

'Marshal Ralph Kirkpatrick. It's him I'm on my way to join.' For a moment her face lit up. 'Mr Pitt, what are we going to do?' She blushed. 'I mean, that is, oh, will you help me? Please. You won't leave me alone here, will you?'

'Of course not.'

'I suppose I could wait for the stage to Felicidad. But with those bodies in there I don't really want to do that.'

'No,' Pitt said. 'That's not a good idea. I think we should be on our way.'

The stage could still be a while in getting here and who knew if the killer would come back? Of course it was also a risk to ride away. The killer could be watching to see if anyone left the stage station. He might have guessed Thora had been present all along and was a witness against him. And might think it worth taking the chance to attack them. But he should be able to handle one man and he decided Thora needed to be got away and quickly.

'Are you going to Felicidad as well?'

'That I am. I saw a spare horse in the corral.' Pitt paused. With her accent and store-bought clothes Thora was obviously from the East. 'That is, I suppose you can ride?'

'Not very well,' Thora admitted. 'But in the circumstances I'll manage. I must get away from here.'

'Let's go out the back way then you won't have to pass the bodies again.'

'All right. Oh, Mr Pitt, my carpetbag.'

25

'Don't worry. I'll get it. Where is it?'

'By the table.'

He gave her hand a comforting squeeze. 'We'll soon be on our way.'

'Good. Thank you. Thank you for helping me.'

Oh dear, Thora thought, once she was alone. What a mess she must look. She raised a shaky hand to her head. Her bonnet was askew and strands of hair had come loose from the bun and were tumbling around her neck. Her face was streaked with tears, eyes puffy, and she couldn't stop trembling. Not in the least like the way she'd hoped to greet Ralph. She told herself off. At least she was alive. Those poor men were dead. One thing she was certain of – the man who killed them wasn't going to get away with what he'd done.

She followed Pitt outside.

CHAPTER FOUR

Old Man Hennessey rode away from the stage station feeling exhilarated, pleased with himself, and worried.

Exhilarated because he'd killed three people. He'd only killed a couple of times before. Once when he was a young man and was confronted by a cowhand who caught him branding calves that didn't belong to him. The second time was during a robbery when the store clerk had foolishly drawn a gun on him and Bobby-Jo. Of course, there was that man who'd died from his injuries after being beaten up by him and Bobby-Jo but that hardly counted. He wondered why he didn't kill more often. It was certainly exciting: watching the fear in his victim's eyes and feeling the power it gave him.

He was pleased with himself because he'd caught up with that damn idiot, Mills. Paid him back for daring to knock him out. He wished he could shoot the silly bastard all over again. He couldn't wait to get his revenge on Lizzie, who was always being unfaithful to him, and maybe Jake Carney himself, who liked stirring up trouble.

But, although he didn't like admitting it even to himself, he was also worried.

Worried because he'd got to tell the rest of the clan: what would they do and say? He expected them to believe he'd done right over the killings and too bad if they didn't, but supposing they heard about what actually went down in Carney's and sniggered at him behind his back?

And he worried most of all because he had shot three people and he had a niggling sensation someone had been present and seen him do it.

Hell! He should have stopped and made sure, not run off like he had because he'd been spooked on hearing a rider approaching. After all he could have shot him dead as well.

He debated whether or not to turn back but decided the stage from Felicidad might be at Freeman's by now and so might the Wells Fargo coach. It was too late. He'd have to trust to luck. And the reputation of him and his family.

Pitt led his horse over to a water trough, letting her take her fill, before going into the barn in search of a spare saddle and bridle. It then didn't take him long to catch up the quietest looking of the horses. Once it was ready he secured Thora's carpetbag to the saddle-pommel and turned to where the girl stood in the shade of the wall.

'You'll have to ride astride,' he told her, beckoning her over.

Thora nodded. That meant hitching up her skirt.

Maybe at another time she might have been too embarrassed to agree but now she was so anxious to get away from the scene of so much death to bother about revealing her legs to a stranger.

Pitt helped her into the saddle and mounted his own horse, patting its neck. As he rode away he kept a careful eye on the surrounding countryside, hand near his rifle.

Thora was still inclined to be tearful and kept shivering. Pitt decided to try to keep her mind off what had happened.

'So, Miss Dowling,' he said, 'where are you from? What are you doing travelling out here on your own? You're obviously a long way from home.'

'I'm going to marry Ralph.' Thora laughed. 'Oh dear! You don't know Ralph, do you? You don't know anything about either of us.'

'No,' Pitt said, with an answering smile.

'Ralph and I both come from a small town back East in Pennsylvania. We were childhood sweethearts.' She blushed shyly. 'Two years ago we decided Ralph should come out West to seek work and when he was established he would send for me.'

'Why was that? What I mean is, why did you want to come to the frontier?'

'I suppose, well, you'll think us both foolish, but, well, we wanted something different. At home we felt stifled. When he finished school Ralph was expected to join his father's business. Mr Kirkpatrick owned a butcher's shop and Ralph simply hated the work. And I was expected to do what my parents said.' Thora sounded as if she'd hated that as well. 'We'd always liked reading stories of the West and we thought it sounded exciting.' Her face saddened. 'I seem to have found more excitement than I bargained for. And quite honestly it wasn't exciting at all.'

'Sometimes it is violent out here,' Pitt admitted. 'But not always.'

'Have you ever shot anyone?' Thora turned in the saddle to look at him.

'No,' Pitt said, although he had done so. But only when there was no other choice. Maybe right now Thora wouldn't want to know that nor appreciate the difference. 'And your Ralph got a job as town marshal in Felicidad?'

'Yes.'

'That seems a strange choice of occupation.'

'Not really.' Thora shook her head. 'You see the law was something Ralph was always interested in. At home he wanted to get a job as town constable before his father begged him to go into the family business. It was only when his father died that Ralph was able to sell the store and follow his dream.'

Pitt supposed town marshal was a reasonably good position, if sometimes dangerous. And it might well involve shooting someone and being shot at. It was certainly hard work for little pay. But Kirkpatrick must have been satisfied he could provide for a wife. He hoped Thora wouldn't be disappointed, in either the marshal's job or the town of Felicidad, which would be quite unlike anything she was used to.

But then every time she mentioned Ralph's name, her eyes lit up, and he thought she was so much in love with him she wouldn't mind what he did for a living; or where he lived.

'And a couple of months ago he wrote asking me to join him,' Thora went on. 'My parents didn't like the idea of me coming to New Mexico. They tried to forbid me! I'm twenty-five.' She sounded most indignant. 'I refused to let them order me around.'

'Why didn't they want you to marry Ralph? Didn't they like him?'

'It wasn't that. They disapproved of our wish to leave our home-town and live on the frontier. Do you understand us?'

'Oh, yeah, only too well. You must have had a long journey.'

'Longer and more tiring than I imagined it would be,' Thora agreed with a little nod. 'Ralph did offer to come and fetch me but I said I could manage on my own.' She sighed, perhaps regretting her decision. 'I soon found that travel out here isn't particularly easy. I seem to have spent as long waiting as actually travelling. But, Mr Pitt, my journey was nearly over. Yesterday I got off the Southern Pacific train at Lordsburg and caught the stage to Mr Freeman's where I was waiting for the connection to Felicidad. And then all this happened.' She gulped, forcing back tears.

'You were certainly unlucky to witness what you did but you'll soon reach your destination. And Ralph.'

Thora tried to smile. 'And you, Mr Pitt, why are you going to Felicidad?'

'I'm going to gamble.'

'Oh!' Thora said wide-eyed. 'You're a gambler?'

31

'That's right.' Pitt was amused, thinking that Thora had never met a professional gambler before and didn't quite know what to make of him.

'Look!' she suddenly exclaimed.

Pitt's hand was scrabbling for his rifle when he realized she had seen the stagecoach from Felicidad coming towards them. With Thora close behind him he rode nearer to the road and held up his hand, hoping the driver wouldn't see them as a threat and would stop.

He did, pulling the horses to a halt in a cloud of dust. The guard sitting beside him pointed a shotgun at them. A couple of passengers, drummers by the look of them, poked their heads out of the nearest window.

Pitt held his hands well away from his sides, not wanting to do anything that might make the guard edgy.

'What is it?' the driver demanded. 'What's the matter?'

'There's been trouble at the stage station.'

'Trouble. What kinda trouble?'

'Three men have been shot dead.'

'What!' Driver and guard stared at one another in shock. 'Are you telling true, mister?'

'Yeah. We've just come from there.' Pitt decided to make no mention of Thora having been a witness. It seemed wise to keep that quiet.

'Not Clint Freeman?' the driver asked.

'Yeah and the boy who worked with him.'

'Hell and damnation! Beg pardon, miss.'

Thora nodded to show she didn't mind.

'Clint. I can't believe it.' The guard shook his

32

head. 'He was one of the good guys. Never had any trouble before. Not even with Indians. He never caused no trouble. D'you know who did it? Or why?'

'No. We're riding into town now to give the marshal the news.'

'Yeah, he'll wanna know.'

'Have you spotted anyone galloping back towards Felicidad?'

'That we ain't.' The guard nudged the driver. 'We'd best be gettin' on out to the station in case the Wells Fargo coach beats us to it. There might be female passengers on their stage and it wouldn't be right for 'em to see the bodies. That is, I suppose you didn't bury 'em?'

'No, I thought it best to get Miss Dowling away.'

The driver nodded. 'OK. P'haps you'd also tell Marshal Kirkpatrick we'll bury the bodies for him. Clint'd want to be buried out there. That place was his life.'

'Oh, the poor man,' Thora said beginning to cry again.

'Don't you fret none, missy,' the guard said. 'Marshal Kirkpatrick is a good lawman. He'll do his best to catch whoever done this. C'mon, we'd better be off. Thanks for the warning, mister.'

'How long will it take us to reach Felicidad?'

'Coupla hours.'

Thora stifled a groan. She really wasn't used to horse riding and her whole body was starting to ache.

'Get to the foothills and you get to the town. Good luck, folks.'

'Thanks.'

*

It was late afternoon when they finally arrived in the foothills of the Mimbres Mountains. The closer they got to the tree-clad slopes the cooler it became, the air filled with the scent of pine. And there in a fold of the land was Felicidad.

They rode through a tiny business district consisting of the stagecoach office, a feed and grain store and a livery stable. And after passing a large Catholic church painted eye-achingly white they came to the centre of the town.

Pitt saw that to go with its Spanish name the town was built in Spanish style with adobe buildings surrounding a plaza, several short streets leading off it. Here were a few stores, a small hotel and on one corner the marshal's office and jailhouse. A number of people were shopping, gossiping, going about important looking business, and the road was crowded with horses, buggies and buckboards.

He glanced at Thora to see how she felt about her new home. She looked too exhausted and scared to bother.

As they rode towards the marshal's office the door opened and a man stepped out.

'Thora!' he cried.

'Ralph! Oh, Mr Pitt, it's Ralph!' And Thora burst into tears, flung herself off her horse and rushed towards the lawman.

CHAPTER FIVE

'Thora,' Kirkpatrick said, gathering her in his arms. 'What's wrong? I was expecting you to arrive on the stage. I was waiting for you.' He stared over her shoulder at Pitt clearly wondering who he was and what he'd done to make his fiancée weep.

Pitt dismounted and caught hold of the reins of both horses, securing them to the nearest hitching rail. He approached slowly. He saw that Ralph Kirkpatrick was about twenty-eight. He was of medium height, not much taller than Thora, with wide shoulders. His brown hair was long and untidy and he had a small moustache and brown eyes. He looked capable, not like an Easterner playing at being a Western marshal who wouldn't be up to handling murder, which was something Pitt had feared.

'And you are?' Kirkpatrick demanded.

Thora pulled away from the shelter of his grasp. 'Ralph, this is Mr Pitt. He helped me. Oh, Ralph, it was awful. I was so frightened.'

'Whatever has happened?' Kirkpatrick sounded

both worried and angry. 'Pitt, what's the meaning of this?'

'Perhaps we'd better go into your office,' Pitt said. 'It would be best if we don't attract attention.' As soon as the door closed behind them and before Kirkpatrick could start bombarding him with questions he added, 'I'm afraid Miss Dowling saw three men get shot.'

'What!' Kirkpatrick was stunned. 'Thora, is this right?'

'Yes. At the stage station.'

'Here, sweetheart, sit down.'

Thora sank down on the chair with a relieved sigh at finding it didn't move beneath her as the horse had. She clung to Kirkpatrick's hand, beginning to feel better now she was with Ralph.

'Pitt, get us all some coffee, would you mind? It's over there. I put fresh on just a while ago.'

'Here, Miss Dowling.' Pitt handed Thora a mug. 'Marshal.'

'Thanks.' Kirkpatrick looked as if he needed something a lot stronger. He ran a hand through his hair. 'Now, Thora, do you feel up to telling me all about it?'

Thora wiped her eyes and nodded.

'Who's dead?'

'Mr Freeman and the boy who worked with him, Jamie. And someone called Adam Mills.'

'Oh, Christ,' Kirkpatrick said, going pale. 'I know Mills. He had a fight with Old Man Hennessey yesterday evening in Carney's Saloon.'

As he spoke Kirkpatrick's heart sank. He bet Hennessey was to blame for the killings: seeking revenge on Mills for besting him in a fight. Obviously Mills hadn't run fast or far enough. And Thora, his Thora, was in the middle of it all.

'The killer was named Bernie,' Thora said.

That confirmed it. Hell and damnation!

'And you saw him?'

'Yes.'

'Oh, Thora.' Kirkpatrick held her close again. 'Sweetheart, I'm so sorry. Did he see you?'

'No, I don't think so. But I'm sure he knew someone was there. He was looking for me.' A tremor ran through the girl.

'And, Mr Pitt, where do you come in?'

'I was heading for the stage station when I heard the shooting from close by and rode to investigate.'

'Did you see the killer?'

'Unfortunately, no,' Pitt said with a little shake of his head. 'By the time I arrived someone was riding away but he was too far off for me to identify either horse or rider.'

'Damn.'

'I take it you know the killer's identity?'

'Only too well. Bernie Hennessey, better known as Old Man Hennessey. Leader of the Hennessey clan. He and his family are a thorn in my side and a thorn in the side of the whole town. Dammit.'

'It's all right, Ralph,' Thora said, putting a hand on his arm. 'It's not your fault.'

But Kirkpatrick thought it was. 'I should have come and met you at Freeman's. The damn local stage is always running late or not running at all. I shouldn't have made you wait out there all alone.'

'I'd travelled all the way from home by myself. I was quite all right up to then. How could you have known what was going to happen?'

'Tell us about the Hennesseys,' Pitt said, filling up the mugs with more coffee.

'Hennessey runs a ranch in the hills.' Kirkpatrick gave a short laugh. 'When I say that I mean it's a ranch of sorts. The family do as little work as possible and run mostly rustled cattle selling them to unscrupulous buyers. They're also known to have committed several robberies. There's the old man, his son, Bobby-Jo, who's as bad as his father, and a married daughter, Belle. Her husband, Charley Burchell, has served two jail sentences over in Arizona. They live out at the ranch as well. I'm not sure what happened to their mother. She was dead by the time I came out here, probably from overwork and ill-treatment. There's also Larry Leapman, their so-called foreman. He and Bobby-Jo are best buddies.'

'Nice bunch,' Pitt said.

'That they are. The local ranchers, led by Thomas Ferguson, are fed up with them. Ferguson ranches in the same area as the Hennesseys. As far as I know he hasn't had any trouble with them. Hasn't said so anyway. Guess Hennessey realizes that if any of Ferguson's cattle go missing he'll be the first suspect. Ferguson employs a lot more men than Hennessey and would be quite willing to string up any rustlers he caught. It's a lot safer and easier to steal cattle from Mexico.'

Pitt glanced at Thora. Her eyes were wide-open

with amazement. She might have read about rustlers and robbers in books but now she was here and they were reality and it was completely different to fiction. Not only that but her husband-to-be was responsible for dealing with them.

'It's suspected, known actually, that both Hennessey and Bobby-Jo have killed before.'

'If you know that why can't you arrest them?' Thora asked, rather indignantly.

Kirkpatrick put an arm around her. 'I wish I could. But there's no evidence against them. Mostly because there's never been a witness to their misdeeds, or at least no one brave enough to stand up in court and testify.'

He glanced at Pitt who realized that Kirkpatrick meant that past witnesses to the Hennesseys' crimes had a habit of being hurt or even disappearing. Wisely Kirkpatrick didn't say so to Thora, not wanting to frighten her more than she was already.

But perhaps he should have spoken up, for Thora said, 'Well, I'm going to.'

'Sweetheart, you can't!'

'Yes I can.' Thora's face assumed a stubborn air, making Pitt want to smile.

'It'll be too dangerous.'

'Ralph, that man shot three people, one a boy of sixteen, as if they meant nothing at all.'

'We'll talk about it in the morning. Who knows, your testimony might not be needed.'

Thora opened her mouth to argue but suddenly all the strength went out of her and she slumped against him.

'I've got you a room at Mrs Barron's boarding house.' Kirkpatrick helped her to stand up, supporting her against him. 'She's a good sort. You'll like her.'

'All I want to do is have a bath, something to eat and sit down in a chair rather than in a saddle.' Thora found she could hardly keep her eyes open.

'Mrs Barron will let you do all three. Mr Pitt, what about you?'

'Don't worry about me. I'll take the horses to the livery then get on down to the saloons.'

'OK, thanks.' Kirkpatrick opened the door and paused to add, 'By the way it'd be best if you didn't tell anyone anything about Thora having witnessed the shootings.'

'I agree. I won't.'

'Good. Thank you for helping Thora.'

'My pleasure. I just wish I hadn't had to.'

So did Kirkpatrick.

He accompanied Thora to the boarding house and telling her he loved her, left her there in the capable hands of Mrs Barron. He thought that probably she would like to be alone for a while, to recover from both the journey and her fear. And he wanted to be alone as well, to think over what had happened. Damn! It certainly wasn't how he'd imagined his first meeting with Thora after all this time apart. He'd been looking forward to seeing her again so much and now all this. What was he going to do about it?

He was torn between his desire to protect Thora and his desire to put Old Man Hennessey in jail – hell, both him and the rest of the bunch out in the hills deserved to be in jail. And he thought himself as less of a lawman because so far he hadn't managed to put them where they belonged.

And he knew from long experience that once Thora's mind was made up nothing he said or did could change it; especially when she knew she was right and especially when it was a matter of justice. He would never be able to persuade her to forget what she had seen.

Thank God Elias Pitt had been there and been willing to help her. Kirkpatrick had recognized Pitt as a gambler. Normally he wasn't any too keen on professional gamblers coming to Felicidad. They often caused trouble and discontent when they won too much.

But in this case he was prepared to make an exception. Besides, Pitt looked trustworthy and honest. Someone who could be depended on. Kirkpatrick entered his office with a little sigh. He had a feeling that in the next few days he was going to need all the help from dependable people that he could get.

CHAPTER SIX

Pitt led the two horses back to the livery stable and left them there, explaining that one belonged to the stagecoach company. He then had to explain what he was doing with it. From the gleam in the eyes of the stable-owner he knew that the story of the killings, and his part in them, would be all around the town before morning. No matter. If there was any trouble from this Hennessey bunch he could always ride away from Felicidad and find another place in which to gamble.

Except that he couldn't. Because he couldn't let Thora Dowling down. He liked Thora. She was a nice young woman. Brave too. Brave to travel all the way out to New Mexico from Pennsylvania by herself and brave to be determined to testify against Hennessey when she could easily have said she hadn't seen anything. Even if people didn't believe her they wouldn't blame her.

And from first impressions he liked Marshal Kirkpatrick too. He and Thora were well matched and deserved a happy life together.

Besides while Pitt didn't seek out trouble, neither

did he walk away from it.

By this time he'd reached the redlight district. He stopped on the corner, taking the opportunity to look about him.

The area wasn't all that large and at this hour of the day wasn't particularly busy, although several horses were tied to railings outside the various buildings. These included three saloons, a couple of brothels, a dancehall and a billards hall. From somewhere came the sound of a tinny piano being played badly and two girls sat on the balcony of one of the brothels displaying ample charms.

And down there that had to be Carney's Saloon where the trouble had started that led to the shooting. Thank God he wasn't going there!

Instead Pitt headed for The Silver Dollar.

The largest and clearly the best of the three saloons, it stood on the nearest corner. Its name was spelt out in fancy gold-leaf lettering on the windows. Swing doors led into a square room with plank flooring, paintings of fights between the US Cavalry and Indians on the walls, and a mahogany bar – goodness knew where that had come from! – behind which were stacked shining glasses. A few customers sat at tables but at the moment no games of chance were going on, although Pitt saw a roulette wheel in the corner. Neither was there any sign of girls, not even behind the bar, although that too might be different in the evening.

While one elderly man was wiping down the empty tables, another stood behind the bar. He looked up as Pitt approached him. He was in his forties, with red hair, green eyes and a florid face as if he indulged in too much drinking. He was dressed flamboyantly.

'Help you?' he said.

'Are you Ned Wilkes?'

'Yes, sir.'

'Elias Pitt. I telegraphed you about getting a job here as a card dealer.'

'Oh yeah.' Wilkes wiped his hands on a piece of cloth and reached across to shake Pitt's hand. 'Pleased to meet you. Like a beer? On the house.'

'Yeah.'

It was cold and frothy and more than welcome. Pitt downed it in a couple of swallows.

'You look like you needed that.'

'I did.'

Wilkes looked curious. He would soon learn about the shooting and perhaps wonder if there was any reason why Pitt hadn't mentioned it. Pitt quickly told the saloon-owner most of what had happened. He left out Thora's part in it as he'd promised Kirkpatrick.

'And Kirkpatrick thinks Old Man Hennessey is the killer, does he?'

'So I believe.'

'Wonder why.'

'I heard Hennessey had a fight with Adam Mills at Carney's Saloon. And was knocked unconscious. Is that right?'

'Yeah, last night. Everyone's talking 'bout it. It was 'bout the only time anyone beat Hennessey in a fight.' Wilkes's face darkened. 'Thinking on it I guess

44

that'd be enough of an excuse for Hennessey to go after Mills. The fool should've ridden away and not stopped till he'd gone too far to be caught up.' He shook his head. 'Damn Jake Carney! Hell, Mr Pitt, my advice to you is keep away from Carney's. I run an honest place here where people can lose their money honestly. Everyone knows that. Ain't nothing honest about Jake Carney.' He glared at Pitt. 'I hope you're honest.'

'Yeah, always.'

'Good, I have a reputation to keep up.' Wilkes paused to serve a customer with a beer then came back to Pitt. 'Perhaps this time Kirkpatrick will go after Hennessey and perhaps if he's lucky he'll make the charge stick. He's certainly as angry as most folks around here about 'em. And frustrated at not being able to lock the lot of 'em up.'

'What's Kirkpatrick like?'

Wilkes gave a little shrug. 'I have as little to do with the law as possible but from the little I do know he seems OK. For an Easterner that is.' He grinned. 'There was some doubt he'd be up to the position being a greenhorn but the Town Council said they'd hire him and give him a chance if he agreed to a lesser wage and one deputy 'til he'd proved himself.'

'And he has?'

'Yeah, he's learned our ways quickly. Settled in well. Keeps the town quiet.'

Having considered Kirkpatrick a good man, Pitt was pleased about that.

'And it ain't his fault the Hennesseys are out there, causing mischief. No lawman's yet been able to do anything about 'em. They were here before he arrived and I expect they'll still be here after he's left.'

'Do they come to town much?'

'No, not often. They know they're not welcome, although that don't bother 'em.' Wilkes rubbed down the already gleaming counter. 'Luckily they don't come in here. They stick to Carney's, and Bobby-Jo and Leapman, that so-called foreman of theirs, sometimes go into the brothel run by the Prices where the girls and what they charge are cheap. That's another place you oughtta keep away from. You want a girl go to the other brothel. That has a reasonably good reputation.'

'I'll bear that in mind.'

'When do you intend to start playing?'

'Tomorrow now. I like to get my bearings first. That OK with you?'

'Yeah sure. Do you want to board here or go to the hotel? There's a room out back I can let you have cheap and I've got a kitchen where I fix up breakfast, although you'll have to go to the café for the rest of your meals.'

'I'll take your room.' Although Pitt normally stayed in hotels he liked to be in the heart of the action when he was gambling.

'I don't have whores working for me and I'd appreciate it if you didn't bring any girls back to the room for the night. Other than that you're free to come and go as you please.'

Pitt nodded agreement. At the moment he wasn't particularly worried about going with a woman and

46

he knew better than to mix business and pleasure.

'It's through here.' Wilkes opened a door at the end of the bar. It led to a corridor and a flight of stairs up to the bedrooms. 'Café will be closed now,' he said, 'but I've got some beefstew left over from my supper last night. You're welcome to share.'

'Fine.'

The bedroom was poky and full of furniture but it was reasonably clean and overlooked the alley at the back of the saloon so it would also be reasonably quiet. Pitt had slept in better rooms and more comfortable beds but he'd also slept in worse. It would do.

CHAPTER SEVEN

'Wonder where Pa is,' Bobby-Jo Hennessey said as he leant against the corral wall. He stared beyond the couple of horses grazing there to the way down through the hills that his father would use on the way home from Felicidad. 'He oughtta be back by now. He was only goin' to stay one day.'

Larry Leapman turned from where he was rubbing down his horse. 'I shouldn't worry. He can look after hisself.'

'I ain't worried.' Not only was Leapman right but the corral wall was broken down in a couple of places. If his father was here he might expect Bobby-Jo to help mend it. And if there was one thing Bobby-Jo didn't like it was hard work; or work of any kind. 'But he was talking 'bout goin' on down into Mexico before it gets too hot.'

The two men looked at one another and grinned. They were both just turned thirty and had known each other for a long time. They were good friends, being two of a kind, and liked the same things. And what they liked most was riding into Mexico where the señoritas made them welcome; where there was cattle to be rustled and driven back to New Mexico to sell to buyers who were unfussy about where the animals had come from, all for an easy profit.

'P'raps if he ain't back soon we'd better ride into Felicidad, find out where he is.' Bobby-Jo didn't much care where his father might be but if Hennessey was in trouble he wouldn't be pleased with the rest of the clan if they made no effort to get him out of it.

'D'you think that stupid marshal has found some reason to carry out his threat to arrest him?'

'Woe betide him if he has.' Bobby-Jo smiled. He'd decided that when the odds were stacked in his favour he'd go up against Kirkpatrick, who being an Easterner would be no match for him. 'But it ain't likely, Kirkpatrick ain't that much of a fool.'

Leapman finished with the horse and came to join Bobby-Jo at the wall. He took a drink from his canteen.

Then looking up he said, 'Hey, looks like he's coming now.' He pointed towards the trail where a faint rise of dust could be seen. He shielded his eyes against the sun. 'Yeah, it's your pa.'

As Old Man Hennessey rode into view, the door to the nearby house opened. Belle and her husband, Charley Burchell, came out, walking together down to the corral. Burchell was slightly shorter than Belle who was almost as tall as her brother.

'Belle don't look too pleased,' Leapman said in an aside to Bobby-Jo.

'She ain't. As usual. She wanted Pa to take her into town and he wouldn't. And Charley agreed with Pa.'

'Charley always does.'

They both laughed. Most people, including them, nearly always agreed with what Old Man Hennessey said but that didn't stop them thinking Burchell was a coward. He had a reputation for violence from his days in Arizona but so far they hadn't seen any evidence of it. How and why Belle had married him neither could understand. But as soon as he arrived at the ranch, on the run and on his way to Texas, Belle had fallen for his good looks. She wanted to marry him and Hennessey had, through threats and force, made sure she got what she wanted. That both she and Burchell, who had little in common, regretted their marriage almost before the ceremony was over was common knowledge and something else for Bobby-Jo and Leapman to snigger over. They thought that Belle wanted to leave Burchell, and Burchell certainly wanted to leave her, but Hennessey was strict where the morals of his daughter were concerned and would never allow that.

'I suppose it must get lonely for Belle stuck out on the ranch most of the time.' For once Bobby-Jo thought of someone else other than himself. 'Looking after the rest of us for no thanks.'

'I don't think it's just that. I think she'd rather be out robbing and rustling with us!'

Belle was as good at riding and using a gun as the men.

'Yeah mebbe,' Bobby-Jo agreed, slapping his friend's shoulder. 'Hey, Pa! You're back at last. Where you been? We expected you last night.'

He glanced nervously at Leapman. Hennessey

looked both angry and excited: not a good combination. Something had happened. And it probably had to do with the bruises on his face. Hell!

Hennessey dismounted. He flung the horse's reins at Burchell, who, while not looking pleased at being treated like a hired hand, nevertheless caught them. He led the horse into the corral and shut the gate.

'Pa, you been fighting again?' Belle said.

'And come off worse by the looks of things,' Leapman whispered to Bobby-Jo who nodded.

'There musta been three or four of 'em,' Bobby-Jo said. 'Or leastways that'll be what he tells us!'

'And of course we'll believe him.'

Bobby-Jo and Leapman grinned until they saw Hennessey glance in their direction.

'Come inside, I'll tell you 'bout it,' the Old Man growled. He pushed by his daughter almost knocking her over. 'Get me a drink, girl. Quick! And I hope you've got some stew on the go. Better have. I'm hungry as well as thirsty.' He strode towards the house, leaving the others trailing in his wake.

They all risked glancing at one another. Now what?

Inside while the four men slumped into chairs in the dim and cool parlour, Belle fetched them all glasses of whiskey and left the bottle on the table. If she, like her husband, felt resentment at being ordered around she didn't dare say anything either. Her father was fond of using his fists and belt. Despite the fact that she was twenty-four and a married woman and Bobby-Jo was six years older, that wouldn't stop him thrashing them if he felt like

51

it. And it was obvious that right now he was near to exploding.

'That's better,' Hennessey said, drinking the whiskey down and wiping his mouth with his hand. 'More, girl. Hurry it up. Fill the glass up this time.'

'What happened?' Belle asked as she quickly did as she was told.

'Had a run in with Adam Mills.'

Mills! Everyone was surprised. Adam Mills wasn't the sort to go up against Hennessey if he could avoid it.

'He give you those bruises?' Bobby-Jo said before he could stop himself.

Hennessey glared at his son, who sank back in his chair wishing he was invisible and hoping he hadn't gone too far.

'You shoulda seen the bruises I gave the other sonofabitch.' Hennessey paused then glared round again, fixing each in turn with his gaze. 'You might hear tales down at Carney's. 'Bout how Mills knocked me out.'

There was a moment of silence, while everyone else sat very still and quiet, not daring to move, hardly daring to breathe.

'The damn stories ain't true. Mills beat me, yeah sure, but only because the sonofabitch tricked me. Hit me from behind.'

'The bastard,' Bobby-Jo said.

He wasn't sure whether he believed his father or not, although as Larry had said, it was wise to act as if he did. Knocking Old Man Hennessey out, whether from behind or in a fair fight, didn't seem a sensible thing for even someone as foolish as Mills to do but his father was so furious something of the sort must have happened.

'The sonofabitch ran out on me but I got him in the end.' Hennessey's eyes glittered and he smiled evilly. He grabbed up the bottle and slurped whiskey from it, some of the liquid spilling down his chest.

'What have you done, Pa?' Belle said.

'Caught up with the bastard at Freeman's and shot him dead.' Hennessey laughed aloud at the memory. ' 'Course I then had to kill Freeman and that kid he had out there too. But what the hell?'

'Pa,' Belle said faintly.

Charley Burchell quickly stifled a gasp. Not for the first time he wondered what the hell sort of family he'd become involved with.

Bobby-Jo felt a mixture of dismay and admiration. Dismay won out. He feared his father had gone too far this time.

'Three men dead,' he said. 'Kirkpatrick ain't gonna like that.'

Hennessey said what Kirkpatrick could do in no uncertain terms.

'Bobby-Jo's right,' Belle said. 'The marshal has it in for you already.'

'He's got it in for the whole family, honey,' Burchell added, not blaming the marshal for that.

Belle ignored him. 'He's bound to suspect you.'

'So what?'

'I guess it'll be OK,' Bobby-Jo said a little uncertainly with a glance at his sister. 'Kirkpatrick might suspect it was Pa shot Mills but he can't prove it. It ain't like Pa left any witnesses.' He looked at Hennessey, who refused to meet his eyes. Oh hell! 'Er, you didn't, did you, Pa?'

'No, I don't think so.' Hennessey spoke in a slurred voice.

'What do you mean by that?' Belle demanded.

'There might've been someone else out at the stage station.' Hennessey would never have admitted that if he'd been sober.

'Don't you know?' Bobby-Jo said. 'Didn't you make sure?' It wasn't like his father to act so stupidly.

'Heard five or six riders approaching the station at a gallop. They musta heard the shots and been coming to investigate. I couldn't wait around for them to catch me, could I?' Hennessey's hands bunched into fists.

Everyone hurried to agree.

'But, hell, I don't see what it matters. Even if someone was there, even if he saw me, how the hell is that goin' to help Kirkpatrick? No one'll ever risk testifying against me.' He laughed again. 'No one's that brave. And hell if Kirkpatrick manages to persuade this witness to agree to speak up before a judge we can always deal with him before it gets to a trial. Ain't that right?' They all nodded.

'I don't see what you're worrying for. Kirkpatrick and the law won't never get the better of me.'

'I hope you're right,' Bobby-Jo muttered.

'Hell sure I am,' Hennessey shouted. He half rose from his chair.

'We can handle this,' Leapman said quickly, trying to calm the man down. 'Like we do everything else.'

Thankfully Hennessey slumped back down.

'Sure we can,' he said. 'You're good to me, the lot of you.' Tears came into his eyes. 'I know I can depend on my kids to help me.'

Bobby-Jo sighed. His father in a maudlin mood was almost worse than in a fury. Luckily it didn't last.

'Now, girl, don't just sit there. Go and get me some food. Me and the boys here have gotta make plans for riding down into Mexico. And enjoying ourselves. And that goes for your husband as well.'

Hennessey stared at Burchell with sly eyes, wanting to cause even more trouble between him and Belle, although he knew as well as the rest of them that Burchell would never dare cheat on his wife.

The sooner they went the better, Bobby-Jo thought. Reach the border and they'd be safe. He could tell from their faces that Leapman and Burchell felt exactly the same. There were times when his father shouldn't be let out on his own and this was obviously one of them.

'Mebbe we can go tomorrow,' he said.

'Yeah, sure, yeah.'

Bobby-Jo glanced at Leapman, who shook his head. From the way Hennessey was drinking whiskey that wasn't likely to happen. Instead he would wake up with a hangover and be in no mood or condition to travel.

CHAPTER EIGHT

Thora woke up to a shaft of sunlight shining in through a gap in the curtains and the sound of movement downstairs in the boarding house.

Goodness, she thought sleepily, it was morning; she had slept the whole night away. She certainly felt refreshed. She sat up and stretched, then lay back down reluctant to leave the bed, which was very comfortable and clean. In fact the whole boarding house was comfortable and kept spick and span. Her room was quite small but very neat and the window looked down on a quiet street with a couple of well-cared for houses on the other side. And Mrs Barron had been kindness itself as Ralph said she would be.

While Thora had unpacked, the woman boiled up enough water to fill the tin bath, which was kept in a room off the kitchen. There Thora had washed away the dirt and exhaustion of the journey and dried herself with a fluffy white towel. Afterwards she found a side-table had been laid in the dining room so she could have dinner without waiting for the other guests. Evidently there were just two others staying at the boarding house at the moment: a young man who worked as a clerk in the bank and a cattle buyer who was visiting the ranches in the area.

While she ate Thora found she could hardly keep her eyes open. And as soon as she'd finished she went to her room and although it was still only early evening had gone to bed. She must have fallen asleep straightaway.

Now she rolled over and reached for her watch, which had been a twenty-first birthday gift from her parents. For a moment she missed her mother and father very much and wished they could have given her their blessing for coming out here to get married; perhaps even accompanied her. At the same time she hoped they never came to hear of what had happened yesterday. All their worst fears about the lawlessness and danger of her new home, and anger at Ralph's stubborness in coming out to New Mexico, would be proven true. Later that day she would have to write to them telling them she'd arrived safely.

Looking at the time, she was shocked to find it was just gone 7 o'clock. Time to get up.

Thora was drawing back the curtains to peer out at the early morning when there was a tap on the door. Thora said, 'Come in,' and Mrs Barron poked her head round the door.

'Ah, Thora, so you're awake,' she said with a smile. 'Did you sleep well?'

'Yes, thank you.'

'Good. Breakfast will be ready in a short while.'

'I'll be down.'

As she washed and dressed Thora thought again

about what she had witnessed at the stage station. It almost felt like a bad dream, although of course she knew it wasn't. What had happened was real enough and it was awful; those poor men. But it had happened and she couldn't change it. And while she would never forget it she must put it to the back of her mind and get on with her life; the life she had come out to share with Ralph.

Downstairs she was greeted politely by her two fellow guests. She joined them at the table and as she sat down Mrs Barron brought in breakfast: scrambled eggs, thickly cut ham, freshly baked and hot biscuits and several pots of coffee. Enough, Thora thought, to feed twenty guests rather than three! But she seemed to have as good an appetite as the two men – perhaps it was the air! She was on her third cup of coffee and was wondering if she should have another piece of ham when Mrs Barron came back in, an enormous smile on her plump face.

'Thora, Marshal Kirkpatrick is here to see you.'

'Oh!' Hastily Thora finished her coffee. Aware of everyone smiling, she blushed, wiped her mouth with a napkin, said a quick, 'Excuse me,' and left the table.

Hat in hand, Kirkpatrick was waiting in the hall-way. Diplomatically Mrs Barron didn't follow Thora but pretended to have work to do in the dining room.

'Sweetheart!' Kirkpatrick caught Thora up in his arms and they hugged and kissed one another. 'How are you this morning?' he asked when at last they drew apart.

'Much better.'

'You look it.'

'Oh, Ralph, I'm sorry for the silly way I behaved yesterday. All those tears. The way I looked. It wasn't how I hoped to arrive in Felicidad. I wanted to look so nice for you. You must think me a terrible ninny.'

'Don't be silly.' Kirkpatrick put his arms round her again. 'You'd had a shock. Your reaction to that was only natural. But it's over now. We can put it behind us. Get on with our lives.'

'Just what I was thinking.' Thora paused for a moment, looking at his suddenly hopeful face as he probably thought she had changed her mind about testifying against Hennessey. Should she? Shouldn't she? It didn't take her long to make up her mind. 'Yes, Ralph, it is over except that I intend to do my duty and tell a court of law what I witnessed.'

'Are you sure you want to?' A frown of worry creased Kirkpatrick's forehead.

'Yes. I won't pretend I'm not frightened. Of course I am. Especially after what you said about Hennessey and his family. But I could never live with myself, or with you, if I didn't do my best to put him behind bars where he belongs. And supposing I kept quiet and he killed someone else? That would be dreadful. He can't be allowed to get away with what he did. I won't let him.'

Kirkpatrick hugged her tightly, proud of her even while he was also scared for her.

'Anyway if he's as bad as you say then I don't think I'd be any safer if I refused to testify. Perhaps less so actually. He'd be aware that I knew what he'd done.

And he would be free to do whatever he liked to me to make sure I didn't change my mind.'

'He need not find out if we pretended you hadn't been there. Only you, me and Pitt know at the moment and Pitt has promised to keep quiet.'

Thora wasn't tempted. She shook her head in determination. 'No, Ralph. Anyway it's bound to come out, sooner or later, that I was there waiting for the stagecoach. You can't keep these things quiet. Remember how it was at home. No secrets were safe there, were they? And I imagine Felicidad is the same.'

'You're right,' Kirkpatrick agreed reluctantly. 'Everyone likes to gossip. Well I won't try to dissuade you. So long as you're aware of the risks.'

'I am. Anyway you'll protect me.'

Kirkpatrick said nothing to that. He hoped he could live up to Thora's expectations. The trouble was she didn't know the Hennessey clan like he and everyone else did.

'What happens now?'

'I'll try to get a few men together and go out and arrest Hennessey. I don't want to face the family with just Dave Vaughan, that's my deputy, for company.'

'A posse?' Thora had read all about posses. 'Will other men go with you?'

'I expect so. I hope so.' Kirkpatrick paused. 'Thomas Ferguson, the rancher I told you about, has promised to let me have a couple of cowboys whenever I need them.'

'Will that be enough?'

'Yes.'

Thora didn't think Ralph sounded too sure. 'Are you going today?'

She found she didn't want to let him go away from her so soon. Not now when there was so much for them to catch up on, a great many things to discuss. She bit her tongue rather than say any more. Ralph had an important job to do, she must allow him to do it. It came first.

'Be best. I don't want to risk Hennessey riding away and hiding out in Mexico until he hopes it all blows over.' The sooner it was all over the better. Kirkpatrick kissed Thora's nose. 'But not just yet. First let me show you the house I've bought us.'

'Oh, yes.'

'It's not very large. Just a couple of rooms.' This was all he could afford on a town marshal's salary.

'Mrs Barron says you're a very important person around Felicidad.' Thora smiled as Kirkpatrick reddened. 'Let me get my bonnet and we'll stroll through town and I'll find out for myself if she's right.'

She was!

Mrs Barron had also said that since his arrival in Felicidad Ralph had told everyone who would listen about the girl he'd left behind in Pennsylvania. And that once he'd sent for Thora he'd been in an agony of waiting for her to make the journey. Thora could see for herself that that was true for it took a long time to walk around the plaza as it seemed nearly everyone wanted to be introduced to her, and to praise their marshal.

'Mrs Barron is nice, isn't she?'

'Yes,' Kirkpatrick said with a little nod. 'She comes from the East and when she was a young woman she was involved in the civil war when she helped care for injured soldiers. Felicidad doesn't have its own doctor, so she's the one everyone turns to when some doctoring is needed.'

Finally they reached a short street near to the Catholic church and there at the end was the house with open country beyond it.

'Do you like it?' Kirkpatrick asked anxiously.

As he said, the house was quite small, standing in its own plot, where Thora quickly decided she could grow both flowers and vegetables. An old cotton-wood tree provided shade. The house was made of adobe and when they stepped inside it was thankfully cool. Being lived in by a busy bachelor the two rooms were untidy and sparsely furnished but she looked beyond that to a time when she was married and the house was clean and full of cheerful things.

'Oh, yes, Ralph, it's lovely.'

Kirkpatrick smiled in relief. He kissed her then said, 'I'll have to be going now. Can I leave you here looking round?'

'Of course.' Thora hid her disappointment. She had wanted to talk to him about curtains and pictures for the walls. New furniture. She kept quiet, instinctively knowing that all that would have to wait.

'If you need any help ask Mrs Barron. You can trust her.'

'All right.'

'And I expect Mr Toombs, who owns the dry goods

store will have most everything you want. Just tell him to put it on my tab.'

Kirkpatrick was on the point of going out of the door when he felt a warning might be in order. He came back to where Thora was counting up the kitchen utensils.

'Look, sweetheart, if I do manage to arrest Hennessey all the while he's in jail it'd be best if you didn't visit me at my office.'

To his relief Thora didn't ask why. She knew it could be dangerous, that maybe Hennessey had caught a glimpse of her at the stage station and if he saw her again he might recognize her. He'd realize that she was the witness willing to testify against him.

'And promise me you'll keep well out of the way if his family come into town.'

'Of course. I don't want to meet up with them if I don't have to. You'll be careful too, Ralph, won't you?' Fear clutched at Thora's heart.

'Yes, don't worry. And, Thora, once Hennessey is in jail I'll have to help guard him and either me or Dave will need to be there, day and night.'

Thora couldn't stop herself looking unhappy about that. Kirkpatrick wasn't pleased either. This wasn't doing much for his love life! It certainly wasn't how he thought he'd be spending his first few days with his fiancée!

'I'm sorry,' he said.

'No, it's all right,' Thora told him. 'I understand. You're Felicidad's marshal, it's up to you to take charge.'

'Hopefully it won't be for long. Once Judge

Corbett gets here, he'll want to hold the trial as quickly as possible.'

'That's good.'

'And then we can be married.'

Thora smiled. 'Will I see you later today?'

'Yes. I'll call on you at Mrs Barron's when I can.'

With that Thora had to be content.

When Kirkpatrick had gone, Thora sat down in the only chair, blinking back tears, thinking that her new life here at Felicidad wasn't going quite how she'd imagined it. She realized she'd been naïve to think it would be perfect.

She liked what she had seen of the town. It was pleasant and the people were friendly. She liked this house and most of all she liked the idea of being Mrs Kirkpatrick and starting a family of her own.

But, oh dear, how she wished Ralph wasn't the town marshal. It seemed so dangerous an occupation. Nothing at all like being the constable back home, where the most dangerous thing the lawman faced was the occasional high spirits on a Saturday night and whose job appeared to consist of being a presence around the place. Here Ralph was up against those who carried guns as a way of life and who were willing to use those guns to kill their enemies.

And supposing Ralph had to shoot . . . kill someone? Would he be able to? How would she feel if he did? For all she knew he might already have done so. It was something they had talked about back home but Thora had never seriously considered it a possibility and she doubted whether Ralph had either.

She sighed. She knew she would have to put on a brave face and not say anything. Ralph obviously liked his job and was good at it.

Doubtless if she asked him to, he would give up the position, perhaps become a farmer or buy a store. But he would no longer be happy. He might come to resent her for making him stop doing what he'd always wanted to do. If she did that to him she risked losing his love.

She would just have to hope this trouble with the Hennesseys would soon be over and that meanwhile nothing happened to Ralph.

Or to her!

CHAPTER NINE

Kirkpatrick found Pitt sitting in The Silver Dollar, practising dealing cards. He pulled up a chair and placing two glasses of beer on the table, sat down opposite him.

'Hi,' Pitt said. 'How's Miss Dowling this morning?'

'Better, thanks. I've left her at our house thinking about things like curtains.' Kirkpatrick smiled wistfully, wishing he was there with her, paused, then said, 'I've got a few men together to ride out with me to the Hennesseys' place so I can arrest Old Man Hennessey.'

'Miss Dowling's still determined to speak up against him?'

'Yes. I was wondering if you'd like to come as well? Seeing as how you were involved.'

Joining posses was not something Pitt usually did. On this occasion he was willing to go along. Word about the shooting and his small part in it had spread throughout Felicidad and all morning the curious had been coming to the saloon and asking him questions. He had quickly become annoyed by all the attention.

'When you going?'

'Now.'

Pitt gathered up the playing cards and drank the beer. 'Count me in.'

He told Wilkes where he was going. Wilkes looked a bit worried as if he was afraid he was about to lose his new dealer before Pitt had even started work but he didn't try to stop him. Together the two men left the saloon, heading for the livery stable where Kirkpatrick said the rest of the men were waiting, horses already saddled.

'How far is it to the ranch?' Pitt asked.

'Couple of hours, I guess. But it's an easy ride up into the hills, cool too.'

'Who else is going with you?'

'My deputy, Dave Vaughan, and a couple of Ferguson's ranchhands. I saw them in town getting ready to ride back to the ranch and they agreed to wait and come with me. There's only two of them as the rest are involved in the spring round-up but it should be enough.'

Pitt wondered whether one of the reasons why Kirkpatrick wanted him along was for an extra gun.

The deputy marshal was an older man, who was quite fat and red faced. The two cowboys looked excited and ready for action.

As they left Felicidad a number of people came up to wish them luck. A couple expressed the hope that Hennessey would resist arrest and be killed in a shoot-out.

'I'll have none of that,' Kirkpatrick warned those riding with him. 'Unless there's no choice. Understand?'

'Yeah, Marshal, don't worry,' Vaughan said for them all.

'You might find it difficult to keep Hennessey alive to wait for his trial,' Pitt remarked as they left the last houses behind and started up a narrow path leading between pine-trees and thick undergrowth.

Kirkpatrick shook his head. 'I don't think so. Feelings are running high, yes, sure, but I doubt there's anyone in Felicidad willing to take part in a lynching. They'll be quite content to wait for the judge to get here, hold a trial and sentence Hennessey.'

'How long will that take?'

'Once Hennessey is in custody I'll telegraph Lordsburg. It then depends on whether Judge Corbett is there or out on his circuit. But he's well aware of the Hennesseys' existence and I expect he'll be as anxious as the rest of us for the old man to stand trial and be sentenced. Get rid of Hennessey and maybe the rest of the clan will move away. At least they'll learn they can't carry on robbing and killing and escape justice forever.' Kirkpatrick glanced at Pitt. 'Corbett is called a hanging judge and in this case I can't see him passing any other sentence. The town knows that as well as me so they'll also know Hennessey will be hanged soon enough.'

'Do you expect trouble from the rest of the family?'

'Yes,' Kirkpatrick said simply and sternly. 'They'll try to break Hennessey out of jail. But I'll be ready.'

Was that boasting on Kirkpatrick's part or did he

mean it? Pitt paused, wondering how the marshal would take what he had to say but thinking it needed to be said because he wanted to know if he could depend on the man riding by his side. 'You being from the East, will you be able to shoot and kill if you have to?'

Kirkpatrick nodded. 'Yes.'

'Sure?'

'Yes, don't worry. People do get shot and killed in the Eastern States, you know.'

'Yeah but it's different when you have to pull the trigger yourself. And I guess it's different being a lawman out here than being a town constable back in Pennsylvania like Miss Dowling said you wanted to be.'

'It is different, yes. And although I haven't told Thora I had to shoot someone soon after I became the marshal.' Kirkpatrick's eyes reflected his memories. 'He was drunk and I didn't want to do it but he drew on me and he wasn't that drunk he'd've missed. It was a case of him or me. I'm not fast drawing my gun but I practice a lot and my aim is accurate.'

'That's all I wanted to know.'

The ride up through the hills was lonely. Every now and then the trees opened out into a valley where the grass was thick and lush and full of flowers. Once they saw some grazing cattle too young to have been rounded up. Kirkpatrick said they belonged to Ferguson's ranch, which was situated on the far side of the hill they were climbing.

'Takes a strong man to ranch in the same area as the Hennesseys,' Kirkpatrick added. 'Nearly there now. Their place is just over the next ridge.'

Pitt noticed that Kirkpatrick, followed by Vaughan and the other two, pulled their rifles from scabbards, ready for any trouble. So Pitt, ready for trouble too, did the same.

The Hennessey place. People were right when they said it could hardly be called a ranch.

For a start no cattle were in sight, although grassy meadows stretched out from the buildings in all directions.

'Ain't rustled none lately,' Vaughan said.

As they rode closer, Pitt saw that the corral was broken down and the barn had sagging doors and holes in the walls. There was a small hut, which looked unused, and situated a little way away was the house, which also appeared to have started out as a hut and been added to haphazardly over the years. It had one door and a few windows with no glass in them and a chimney from which smoke rose. To one side someone had once started a vegetable garden but the plants looked as if they were either dying or were already dead.

'Someone's home,' Kirkpatrick said, nodding towards the smoke.

'There's two or three horses in the corral too,' Pitt added.

'Let's hope Hennessey is here.'

'Yeah, Marshal, he is, there he is,' Vaughan said nodding towards the house.

Clearly although Hennessey had just murdered three people he felt so secure he didn't see the need to run away. Or maybe the reason was because he

70

couldn't. For as the posse rode up to the house, the man came out into the open. He looked pale and ill and walked on shaky legs. Pitt, having had one or two hangovers in his younger days, recognized all the signs. Hennessey was suffering a humdinger!

The rest of the family gathered behind him.

'That's Bobby-Jo and Belle,' Vaughan said to Pitt.

Bobby-Jo was as tall as his father but skinny with dark brown hair, balding slightly in the front, and brown squinty eyes. His sister also had brown hair, unflatteringly scraped back from her face into a tight bun, and her mouth was little other than a thin line.

'Next to Belle is her husband, Charley Burchell. He fancies himself as a bit of a dandy but while he'd also like to be considered a ladies man he don't dare do nothing 'bout it since he married Belle. Old Man Hennessey'd have his hide iffen he cheated on his daughter.' Vaughan looked round. 'Wonder where Leapman is. He's usually with Bobby-Jo.'

While Hennessey slumped against the doorpost, Bobby-Jo pushed his way to the front.

'What you doin' here?' he demanded. 'What d'you want?'

'Got a warrant here for the arrest of your pa,' Kirkpatrick said.

'What for?' Belle said.

She glanced at her brother and Pitt thought they both knew only too well what Hennessey had done.

'The cold blooded shooting and murder of Adam Mills . . .'

'That damn trouble-maker,' Belle snapped.

'. . . Clint Freeman, and the boy, Jamie.'

71

Bobby-Jo gave an unconvincing laugh. 'Hell, Marshal, Pa was here all day yesterday.'

'Did I say the shooting took place yesterday?'

'You fool, Bobby-Jo.' Belle aimed a kick in her brother's direction. 'Shut up!'

'Hennessey, we don't want any trouble. Just come with us now.'

'You can't arrest Pa for no reason!' Belle said stridently. 'Who says he done it? You've always got it in for us. We get the blame for everything when we ain't done nothing.'

'No, you're a family of complete innocents, I know.' Kirkpatrick jigged his horse forward. 'Hennessey, let's go.'

'Pa ain't going nowhere.' Bobby-Jo went to draw his gun. He stopped when Kirkpatrick raised his rifle and pointed it at him.

'Don't be stupid,' the marshal said. As Vaughan rode up to join him, he dismounted and strode up to Hennessey.

Out of the corner of his eye, Pitt glimpsed movement at the side of the house. A man, Leapman the foreman probably, stood there, gun out and ready to fire.

Pitt spurred his horse forward, freeing one foot from the stirrup at the same time. Even as Leapman looked up in surprise, Pitt kicked out hard. First at the gun which flew from the man's grasp and then at the man himself. Leapman was sent stumbling to the ground. Pitt rode closer to him so that Leapman quickly rolled away, scared the horse would trample him.

'Stay there,' Pitt ordered. 'Stay down.'

'You won't get away with this,' Leapman said. 'The Hennesseys stick together.' His eyes narrowed. 'I don't know you, do I? You're new to Felicidad. You clearly ain't aware of our reputation. My advice to you is stay away from all this. Ride away while you can.'

'Funny, but I rarely follow other people's advice, especially when I've got the drop on 'em.'

'You can't take Pa,' Belle was screaming.

She went to attack Kirkpatrick but Burchell pulled her away so she contented herself with struggling with her husband, punching and kicking at him.

'Come on.' Kirkpatrick caught hold of Hennessey's collar and quickly secured the man's hands with handcuffs.

One of the cowboys had ridden back to the corral and now returned, leading a horse.

'Get on it.' Kirkpatrick pushed Hennessey towards the animal.

'I ain't done nothing.' Suddenly Hennessey seemed to recover his wits and, realizing the trouble he was in, spoke for the first time. 'You can't arrest me for nothing,' he whined. 'I ain't goin' with you.'

'Yes, you are,' Kirkpatrick said and heaved the man up into the saddle.

'Bobby-Jo, help me! Don't let the bastards take me, your Pa. Stop 'em.'

Pitt joined Vaughan in pointing their rifles at Bobby-Jo, who glared at them but made no move to help his father.

'They'll shoot me before we get to Felicidad.'

73

'No, we won't,' Kirkpatrick said. 'Not if you behave yourself.'

'Don't worry, Pa, we'll come and get you out,' Bobby-Jo snarled.

'Let's go.'

'You won't get away with this!' Bobby-Jo's voice followed them as they rode away while Belle began to scream.

'My boy'll get you all.'

'Shut up, Bernie,' Kirkpatrick ordered.

CHAPTER TEN

'Pa, they've taken Pa!' Belle's voice rose into a screech of anguish. 'How dare they? And you three cowards stood there and did nothing to stop 'em!'

'We were outnumbered and outgunned, honey,' Burchell said in an effort to calm her down.

'Don't you honey me!' Belle turned on her husband. Her hands clawed at his face so he was forced to grab at her to fend her off. 'You let them take him. You just stood there, you weasel!'

'Don't worry, Belle, they won't get away with this,' Bobby-Jo promised. 'We'll get Pa out of jail.'

'You'd damn well better.'

Brushing down his jacket, Leapman joined them. 'Who was that one got the drop on me? Ain't seen him before. Have any of you?'

'No,' Burchell said with a shake of his head.

'It won't be difficult to find out who he is,' Bobby-Jo said. 'Then he'll get what's coming to him, the same as Kirkpatrick will get his.'

As they trooped back inside out of the sun, Belle said, 'Wonder what made Kirkpatrick dare come out here and arrest Pa? He ain't never done so before.'

'He was guilty,' Burchell pointed out, earning himself another glare from his wife.

'Pa thought someone else was out at the stage station.' Bobby-Jo threw himself down in his chair. 'He musta been right. He musta been seen. Kirkpatrick's got hisself a damn witness.'

'Yeah that makes sense.' Leapman looked up from where he was pouring out whiskey for them all.

'Who would dare speak up against Pa?' Belle said.

'Perhaps it was someone who arrived on the stage and who don't know your reputation and so ain't scared of you,' Burchell suggested.

'Could be,' Leapman agreed thoughtfully. 'Well, don't worry, we can ask around. Someone'll know.'

'Yeah we'll ride into town tomorrow . . .'

'Why not now?' Belle demanded.

'Because we need to make plans,' Bobby-Jo told her. Although he didn't say so, he also thought it might do their father good to spend the night in a jail cell; to reflect on where losing his temper and killing three men had put him.

Thora sat with Mrs Barron in the boarding house's parlour. She was sewing hems on the curtains the woman had helped her choose that morning. She had been very surprised and pleased at the goods for sale in Mr Toombs's store. There seemed to be everything a frontier wife could need. And Mr Toombs said that if she couldn't find what she wanted he would order it for her and it would soon arrive by pack train.

Thora's mind wasn't on the task and Mrs Barron

was afraid the hems weren't going to be in the least bit straight!

Because her mother was far away, Thora had confided in Mrs Barron over her part in the shootings. To her surprise the woman hadn't been shocked but then she told her she had seen more than her fair share of the dead and badly wounded during the Civil War. Little shocked her after that.

It was the middle of what Thora considered a very long afternoon when a neighbour put her head round the door.

'The posse is back,' she said in an excited voice.

Thora half rose from her chair.

'No, remember what Mr Kirkpatrick said.' Mrs Barron stood up. 'You wait here. I'll go. I'll be as quick as I can.' And with her neighbour she hurried out, leaving Thora alone.

The girl put the curtains down. How could she even think of sewing when Ralph might have been hurt? Oh, what was happening? She went to the window but couldn't see anything. It wasn't fair to expect her to stay here. Doing nothing. She must go out and see. Surely it couldn't do any harm if she kept to the back of the crowds.

She turned, was halfway across the room when the door opened and Mrs Barron came in. The woman was smiling.

Thora let out the breath she didn't know she'd been holding.

'Mr Kirkpatrick is quite safe.' Mrs Barron said, holding out her hands to her. 'And they've got Old Man Hennessey with them as their prisoner!'

'Thank God.' Thora sat down abruptly.

'There, I told you everything would be all right, didn't I?'

'Yes,' Thora said with a shaky smile.

'I know this all seems frightening at the moment and dangerous for your Ralph.'

Thora nodded. Mrs Barron was right about that!

'But truly, dear, it's most unusual. Mostly the marshal's job is very ordinary and doesn't involve people like the Hennesseys. In fact, I don't believe there's been above two real miscreants locked in the jail cells since he was appointed to the position. Except for some drunken cowboys of course.'

Thora marvelled at how matter of fact Mrs Barron sounded. Back home her neighbours would have been disgusted about drunken young men and called for a ban on alcohol. But then she reflected that was one of the reasons she and Ralph had decided to come West and seek a freer way of life.

'Now why don't I go and get us a nice cup of coffee and a piece of apple pie each? And then perhaps I'll help you unpick those curtains!'

Thora looked down at her shoddy workmanship. The hems were all over the place. She could hardly put them up at the windows! 'Oh dear,' she said with a laugh.

When Kirkpatrick and the posse reached Felicidad with their prisoner, a crowd turned out to watch. There were even a few jeers but most people stood in silence, pleased at the sight of Old Man Hennessey in handcuffs. Although three men had been killed, they

78

were thankful he would soon be locked up and hoped there would be enough evidence against him so Judge Corbett could sentence him.

By now Hennessey was more or less recovered from his hangover. He'd moaned the whole journey, about how the handcuffs were too tight or he felt sick; protested his innocence. Riding through the streets he scowled round at everyone, made more furious still when no one seemed particularly scared of him. He'd make them scared all right.

At the jailhouse, the two cowboys rode away. And Pitt and Vaughan drew guns on Hennessey while Kirkpatrick helped him off his horse. He pushed the man inside where he freed him of the handcuffs. He opened the door to the small cell-block.

'Get in there.'

'You ain't gettin' away with this!' Hennessey threatened. 'My boy'll have me out afore it gets dark. Then you watch yourself. You see.'

'Yes OK, we will see.' Kirkpatrick shoved Hennessey into the nearest cell.

'You're a dead man! You're all dead!'

Kirkpatrick slammed the door shut on the man, drowning out his voice.

'God,' he said. 'I'm beginning to wish he had tried to escape while we were bringing him in and I could've shot him.'

Pitt and Vaughan grinned.

'Dave, you wait here while I go and telegraph Lordsburg.'

'Marshal, how we going to manage with just the two of us?' Vaughan asked. 'Hennessey will need watching and we'll need to be ready for the rest of the clan causing trouble.'

'I'll try to deputize a couple of men to help us. It's a shame Ferguson is away right now or he'd have let some of his men help. Pitt, I suppose you . . .'

Pitt held up his hands. 'No way, Marshal. I'm not about to wear a badge and walk the streets delivering tax notices. Nor am I about to sit in here all day guarding your prisoner.' But he'd taken an instant dislike to the Hennessey family and their hangers-on and he had also made an enemy of them. Knowing he might in turn want Kirkpatrick's help, he added, 'But if there's anything else I can do just ask.'

'OK.'

'What happens if Bobby-Jo does try to break his Pa out?' Pitt asked.

'He won't succeed. The jailhouse is a fairly new building and it's stoutly constructed.' Kirkpatrick looked round. 'In here there's just the door and one window so it can be easily defended.'

'What about out back where the cells are? Ain't you got a yard where the prisoners can exercise?'

'Yeah, we have.' Vaughan nodded agreement.

'And anyone determined to do so could easily scale the wall,' Kirkpatrick added. 'But each cell has only a tiny window that even a child would find it impossible to get through. And the door to the yard is hefty and is secured with a bar.'

'Could the building be set on fire?' That seemed to Pitt to be about the only way anyone could break in.

'Not easily. The whole place is made of adobe and

while I suppose the doors will burn, by the time they caught alight the alarm would be raised.'

'And help would arrive?'

'I hope so. While people are scared of the Hennesseys I'm sure that in any real trouble most would stand by me. Especially now Hennessey is in jail and doesn't look so big and unstoppable after all. He looks ordinary. And you saw how people reacted to him today. They won't want him breaking out.'

Pitt grinned. 'Well, if you want me you know where I am.' As he went to stand up the door opened and a young woman came in.

She was in her early twenties, with dark, almost black hair and dark eyes. She had a nice figure and would have been quite pretty were it not for the fact that she had bruising all round one eye and her mouth was badly swollen. From the look of her and her clothes, and the way she ran an experienced eye over him, Pitt had no doubt she was a prostitute. And someone had beaten her up.

'Hallo, Lizzie,' Kirkpatrick said.

Lizzie. Pitt thought that was the name of the girl who had caused the fight between Hennessey and Mills. He sat down again.

'Carney give you those?' Kirkpatrick nodded at her bruised face, confirming what Pitt thought.

Lizzie didn't answer but tried to look as if she didn't know what the marshal was talking about.

Kirkpatrick sighed. 'What can I do for you?'

'I want to see Bernie.'

'Whatever for?'

Kirkpatrick and Pitt glanced at one another, while

from his corner Vaughan sighed.

'Because . . .' Lizzie bit her swollen lip and clenched her hands together to prevent them shaking. 'Well, he'll get off, won't he? That is even if he stands trial, which Mr Carney says he won't. So when he does go free I want him to remember I came here to visit him and didn't forget 'bout him.'

'He will stand trial and he will be convicted.'

'So you say, Marshal. Mr Carney says otherwise.'

'Blast Mr Carney. You don't have to believe everything he tells you.'

Lizzie went on as if Kirkpatrick hadn't spoken. 'Mr Carney says Bernie blames me for Adam hurting him. And he says it's my fault Bernie's in jail.' Tears came into the girl's eyes and she brushed them away. 'Even if I'm real nice to him he'll give me more of this.' She touched her mouth. 'I don't want to make it any worse.'

'Hell, Lizzie, why don't you leave Carney? He's bad news. And Hennessey is worse. You can do better for yourself than working for the likes of them. Ride away from Felicidad while you've got the chance. Now while Old Man Hennessey is locked up and the rest'll be too concerned about him to come after you.'

For a moment the girl's face lit up with hope which quickly died.

'Where would I go? What would I do? I ain't got no money. And you know Carney wouldn't let me go. He'd catch me and this'd be nothing to what I'd get then.' She took a deep breath. 'Can I see Bernie now? I ain't bringing him a weapon or nothing like that.'

'Yeah go on through. Dave, go with her, make sure she doesn't try anything.'

'I won't, you needn't worry. I don't want to help him, only myself.'

'Yes I know but if you're alone with Hennessey he'll expect you to try to break him out. With Dave there Hennessey will know there's nothing you can do.'

'Yeah, Marshal, thanks.' Lizzie gave him a small smile.

When she'd gone, Pitt said with an edge of anger in his voice, 'I don't hold with men who beat up girls.'

'Do you think I do?' Kirkpatrick was just as angry. He scowled at Pitt as if he thought the man was accusing him of not helping Lizzie because she was a prostitute. 'Jake Carney is a brute. You heard what Lizzie said. She's right. A little while after I was made marshal he half killed one of his girls when she tried to run away.'

'What did you do?'

'Nothing. Because she, like Lizzie, was too scared to give evidence against him. Carney knows that and he knows he's bought the backing of the Hennesseys. He just smirks at me when I accuse him of anything.' Kirkpatrick shook his head. 'I'd like to help Lizzie really I would. Unfortunately there's nothing I can do.'

CHAPTER ELEVEN

It seemed to Pitt that the whole town was holding its breath. Waiting.

The previous evening not many men came into The Silver Dollar and those who had wanted to talk about the situation, not gamble. Profits were slim. But as Wilkes pointed out if and when Hennessey's trial took place the whole town would be buzzing, both during the trial and afterwards when people were waiting for the hanging.

The next morning when Pitt went out for a walk round the plaza, he noticed that although it was a lovely day, warm but not yet hot, not many people were abroad. Women scurried about their shopping eager to get it done so they could go home and shut their doors while the few men on the streets all wore guns on their hips.

There wasn't long to wait.

It was early afternoon when Bobby-Jo and the rest of the Hennessey clan rode into town. They galloped towards the marshal's office, shouting and yelling. Despite staying up late the previous night, thanks to drinking a couple of bottles of whiskey they hadn't managed to make any plans beyond using force and plenty of gunfire to break Hennessey out of the jail-house. This would be followed by riding away and heading for Mexico where they would be safe. None of them had any doubts that they would get away with it; no one in Felicidad would dare stand up against them. Anyone foolish enough to try would be shot and killed. And that included the marshal who anyway would doubtless scurry off, tail between his legs at the first sign of danger.

So when they reached the jailhouse they were extremely surprised to find not only Kirkpatrick on the sidewalk outside, shotgun held firmly in his hands, but his deputy, Vaughan, behind him, also holding a shotgun. And both of them looked deter-mined.

'Hold steady,' Kirkpatrick said to Vaughan, who nodded.

The clan came to a confused halt by the side of the road. That the marshal and his no-account deputy would stand up to them was the one thing they hadn't expected.

'Hold it right there,' Kirkpatrick called. 'Bobby-Jo, I don't want any trouble but your pa is staying in jail to await Judge Corbett. So why don't you all ride away while you can?'

'Hell, Marshal, you can't hold a Hennessey.' Bobby-Jo spoke with as much bravado as he could, even while he was hoping Kirkpatrick didn't decide to use the shotgun. From the corner of his eye he saw Mr Toombs with several other men waiting in the doorway of his store. Were they just watching or would they help their marshal? He didn't want to take the chance on finding out.

'We'll see about that.'

'What shall we do?' Leapman asked.

'Why don't you charge 'em?' Belle demanded. 'There's only two of 'em and one is an Easterner! We can beat 'em easy. They won't shoot at us.'

'You don't know that,' Burchell said. He caught hold of the reins of her horse to stop her doing anything silly. 'They look quite ready to shoot to me.'

Belle scowled at her husband as if she'd like to shoot him herself.

'Charley's right.' For once Leapman agreed with Burchell. 'The bastards've got the drop on us. Ain't nothing we can do, not right now.'

'Not one of you is prepared to die for Pa.'

They didn't answer Belle; she was quite right!

'Well, what is it to be?' Kirkpatrick demanded. 'This shotgun is getting heavy and my trigger finger's getting itchy.'

'OK, OK,' Bobby-Jo said sulkily. 'We're goin'. But you ain't seen the last of us. You'll pay for this, all of you.' To his surprise neither man looked worried. Perhaps they had also seen Mr Toombs and his friends. 'Just remember you can't guard Pa all the time.'

'Yes, I can. Go on, go. All of you.'

'Wait!' Belle cried, stopping the others from riding away.

'Belle, don't,' Burchell said.

'It's OK, Charley, I ain't goin' to do anything stupid.' She turned back to Kirkpatrick. 'Marshal,

86

can I come in and talk with Pa? Make sure he's OK. I promise not to do anything I shouldn't.'

Kirkpatrick wasn't very happy with the idea but he didn't see how he could prevent a daughter visiting her father. At least Bobby-Jo didn't seem inclined to want to join her. He nodded. 'Just you then.'

'Belle,' Burchell said again, a little uncertainly this time.

She swung down from her horse. 'Don't worry about me,' she told him impatiently. 'You go with Bobby-Jo and Larry. Get drunk. That's what the three of you do best.'

'Come on.' Bobby-Jo didn't intend to wait around any longer when there was the possibility of getting shot. He dug spurs in his horse's sides and, followed by Burchell and Leapman, galloped away towards the redlight district and Carney's saloon.

Kirkpatrick watched them go with a little sigh of relief. That was the first crisis over and both he and Vaughan had stood firm. He nodded across the road towards Mr Toombs who nodded back.

Looking furious with both her family and the marshal, Belle tied her horse to the hitching rail and stepped up onto the sidewalk. Kirkpatrick opened the door and Vaughan stood aside to let her through, then quickly took up his place outside again.

'I'll have to ask you to hand over any weapons you're carrying.'

Belle tutted crossly. She wore a holstered Colt .45 round her waist and she placed this, and a small derringer she had in the bag she was carrying, on the marshal's desk.

'Is that all?'

'Yeah.'

Kirkpatrick held out his hand and reluctantly Belle gave him her bag. He peered inside and with a tut of his own pulled out a knife.

'Oh dear,' Belle said. 'I forgot all about that.'

'Sure you did.'

'So, Marshal dear, d'you want to search me as well as my possessions?'

'Yes.' Kirkpatrick almost smiled at Belle's look of shock and fury. 'Hold out your arms while I pat you down.'

'No!'

'Do it or don't go in to see your pa.'

Her face mutinous, Belle did as she was told. 'No funny business,' she said.

'No problem. You're not my type.' Kirkpatrick quickly made sure she had no more weapons about her. 'OK, Mrs Burchell, you can go on through.'

'My bag?'

'That stays here with me. Go on. Don't stop too long.'

Not quite sure what to expect, Belle opened the door to the cells. She wasn't certain why she had insisted on visiting her father. She didn't love him, love wasn't an emotion that meant anything to any of the Hennesseys; she didn't even like him much. He was a bully and if anything she was scared of him and his uncertain temper. But all her life she had been taught that the Hennesseys stuck together, that it was them against everyone else. She had also quickly learned that what the family wanted they took with no one and nothing to stop them. That had always been the way of things up till now. Now here was her father in jail, awaiting trial for murder and Kirkpatrick wasn't taking any notice of their threats, nor would he release him. It just wasn't right!

'Pa?'

'Girl, is that you?' Hennessey came to the door of his cell and clutched at the bars so hard his knuckles turned white. 'You come to get me out?'

'Not yet. But I have come to see if you're all right.'

Hennessey scowled. 'Of course I ain't all right. Don't be so stupid. I'm in a jail cell. How can I be all right?' He looked beyond her and scowled even harder when he saw she was alone. 'Where's your damn brother and Larry? Ain't they with you? They'll set me free even if you ain't goin' to bother. Why ain't you busting me out right now?'

'The damn marshal got the drop on us.'

'And you let him? Some damn Eastern green-horn?'

'But Bobby-Jo will come up with a good plan, you can bet on that.'

Hennessey didn't reply. He knew, as well as Belle, that his son's plans never amounted to much.

'Pa, they treating you properly? Giving you enough to eat? Letting you sleep?'

'I've had a couple of meals, yeah. But the food ain't up to much and the bunk ain't real comfortable. The damn marshal won't even let me have any whiskey! All I've had to drink is coffee. Anyway, girl, how the hell d'you expect me to eat or sleep when I'm in here? Waiting a trial for murder in case you

89

ain't realized. In front of Judge Corbett.' Hennessey closed his eyes for a moment. 'He's a hanging judge. You all know that, don't you? He'll hang me.'

'Oh no, I'm sure . . .'

'You mean you'd like me to be sentenced to a life of hard labour?'

'No, of course not. I meant you'll be in Mexico long before the judge gets here. Don't worry, Pa. It won't ever come to a trial.'

'Supposing it does?'

Belle's heart skipped a beat. Her father not only looked worried, he looked . . . frightened. She'd never seen him frightened of anything before. It was usually everyone else that was frightened of him.

'A jury will never dare find you guilty. They'll be too scared. They know what'll happen to 'em if they do.'

'A lot of good that'd do me.'

'You'll be free soon.'

'You'd better be right.' Hennessey took several turns round his cell. 'I don't like being locked up. I couldn't stand being locked up behind bars in some hell-hole for the rest of my life. But I don't wanna hang.' Fear and panic came into his eyes. 'Girl, you and your brother must get me out. You must, d'you hear?'

'We will, Pa, I promise. Whatever it takes.' Belle stepped up to the bars and put out a hand to him.

Hennessey took no notice. 'You'd damn well better,' he snarled.

With a little sigh, Belle turned away. Even now he wanted nothing from her except her help. Not both-

90

ering to say goodbye she went outside to where Kirkpatrick waited.

'You just treat Pa properly,' she said. 'Or you'll answer to me and Bobby-Jo.'

'I treat all my prisoners properly no matter who they are.'

Belle scowled at him, looking very like her father as she did so.

'There's nothing more for you here,' Kirkpatrick told her. 'Go on home.'

'Not without Pa.'

'You'll be waiting a long time then.'

'Damn you, Marshal.'

Belle left the office, slamming the door behind her and kicking out at the sidewalk.

She was in a raging temper, with everything and everyone, and hardly knew what to do with herself. She was aware that the people around the plaza were looking at her and she was tempted to get into a fight with one of them who would fight her back. Right then she understood why her pa had shot Adam Mills and wished she could shoot someone. She came to a halt on the corner, breathing heavily in an effort to calm down. Losing her temper, doing something silly and getting herself arrested would do no good. One of the clan had to keep a steady head, and the only person that could be was her. The rest wouldn't bother. In fact, she thought, almost everything to do with the family and the ranch was up to her. And if anything went wrong with either she was the one who got the blame.

With that in mind, she decided that while she was

in Felicidad she might as well go to the dry goods store and buy some more whiskey. They only had one bottle left and that wouldn't last long. And some ammunition.

Afterwards if the others hadn't put in an appearance, and she didn't suppose they would have done, she'd go down to Carney's, find out what they were up to. Without her to keep an eye on them Bobby-Jo and Larry, and that useless husband of hers, would doubtless get drunk and probably decide to pay the girls at Price's brothel a visit. Charley had better not accompany them there! She'd have his hide if he did.

She'd be the only one to remember they were in Felicidad to help their pa, not have a good time.

CHAPTER TWELVE

Certain that Bobby-Jo and the others would ride into town as soon as possible to free Old Man Hennessey, Lizzie was watching out for them.

So when the saloon door opened and Bobby-Jo, Leapman and Burchell entered Carney's, she slipped out of the door leading to the bedrooms. At least they couldn't have freed Hennessey because if they had then he would either be with them or they'd all be hightailing it out of town back to the ranch. Had they managed to see him? If so they would have learnt that he'd decided it was her fault he'd shot Adam Mills and was now in jail. Having no minds of their own, and wanting to keep on Hennessey's good side, they would then blame her as well. She could expect no better treatment from them than she could from Bernie.

She cursed the day her looks and figure had caught Hennessey's eye. Being considered his property had caused her nothing but trouble and pain, especially while Carney expected her to continue working for him.

Breathing a little sigh of relief she hadn't been spotted, Lizzie let herself out into the filthy yard at the back of the saloon. If she crept close to the open window near to the bar she might hear most of what was said. That way, hopefully, she would find out what Bobby-Jo and the others were up to and whether she was in any immediate danger. If she was what would she do? What was she going to do anyway? She couldn't hide from them forever. And once Bernie got out of jail he would certainly come looking for her.

'Hey, Jake, three whiskies,' Bobby-Jo demanded as he and the other two bullied their way up the bar. Not many people were in the saloon at this time of day and he stared round at those who were, wondering if there was any one present he could start a fight with; unfortunately they all looked as if they would be able to fight back.

'And make it real quick,' Leapman added.

'Hello, boys,' Carney said. 'Here you go. First ones are on me. You seen your Pa, Bobby-Jo?'

'No, not yet.' Bobby-Jo's face twisted in an ugly frown. 'We came to break Pa out but that sonofabitch, Kirkpatrick, has got the jail sealed up real tight. He agreed to let Belle in to talk to Pa but not the rest of us.' He paused and added in a whine, 'There weren't nothin' for us to do.' He wondered what his father would say and do when he found out his son had failed him yet again.

'Well, Kirkpatrick ain't a fool. Even if he's from the East. And he's got everyone riled up agin you all. He's determined your Pa is gonna stand trial.'

Carney shook his head. 'I can understand Bernie shooting Adam Mills. Mills was asking for it and probably no one would've taken much notice, but it was foolish of him to shoot Clint Freeman and that kid. Freeman was popular around here. People ain't about to forgive and forget.'

Bobby-Jo said nothing. He didn't really understand what Carney meant because he'd never been popular with anyone.

'It was Lizzie's doing, talking to Adam in the first place when she knew Bernie was still in town.' Carney was eager to shift blame from himself.

'What we goin' to do?' Leapman asked. He downed his drink and held out his glass for Carney to refill.

The others did the same but no one offered to pay. Carney hid an annoyed sigh. The Hennesseys only paid if they were flush with money after a profitable rustling trip.

'I dunno,' Bobby-Jo admitted. 'The jail's too heavily guarded for us to rush.' He was pleased when neither of the other two disagreed with him. He didn't really want to risk his life to save his father's. 'What about Judge Corbett? He'll come here from Lordsburg, won't he? Can't we do something to stop him? Kill him perhaps?'

Both Leapman and Burchell looked horrified, while Carney wondered if he could pretend he hadn't heard. Bobby-Jo came up with some weird ideas at times and that was one of the worst he'd ever had.

'Bobby-Jo, we can't go around killing judges,'

Leapman said firmly.

'Who would know it was us?'

'Don't be stupid. Who else but us would want to kill the judge when he's on his way to try a Hennessey? We do something like that we'd not only have the law after us, they'd probably send the army in pursuit as well.'

'They couldn't cross the border after us.'

'Yeah, they could.'

'Larry's right,' Burchell said.

Not for the first time he wondered how he'd become involved with Belle and her family. They were all as bad as one another; stupid as well as wild. He regretted the day he'd decided to seek shelter from the law at the Hennessey ranch and regretted even more that Belle had been attracted to him. Once she'd made known her intention to marry him he should have got on his horse and ridden away and not stopped until he reached Texas. But at first he'd felt flattered that Belle wanted him and then suddenly it was too late: Old Man Hennessey had made sure the marriage went ahead. He was trapped because Hennessey had told him what would happen if he ran out on Belle or did anything to upset her.

' 'Sides,' he went on, 'if Corbett was killed, another judge would only be sent in his place. We can't kill every judge in New Mexico!'

Bobby-Jo scowled even harder. He didn't like being told what to do. Especially by Charley Burchell. But he supposed the others were right.

'OK, forget that. Perhaps you two can come up with a better idea?'

Carney ran a dirty piece of rag along the bar. He leant forward and with a grin on his foxy face said, 'I might be able to help you there, gentlemen.'

'What d'you mean?' Bobby-Jo asked.

'Word is out that Marshal Kirkpatrick has a witness to the shootings.'

'Tell us something we don't already know.' Bobby-Jo reached across and took hold of Carney's collar giving him a threatening shake. 'Or don't waste our time.'

Carney freed himself of the grip. 'Ah, yeah, but I think I know who it is. That's something you don't know, ain't it?'

The other three looked at one another.

'Who?' Leapman asked.

'Word is also out that Kirkpatrick's fiancée, a gal he knew from back East, arrived in Felicidad on the very day of the shootings.'

'A gal?' Leapman said.

'Yeah, why not?'

'So?' That was Bobby-Jo, slow on the uptake as usual.

'But that ain't all. She rode into town with that new gambler working down in The Silver Dollar.'

'Who's that?'

'Dunno his name. But he's hand in glove with the marshal. Even went out with that posse Kirkpatrick led when he arrested your Pa.'

Leapman's hand slammed down on the bar, causing it to wobble alarmingly. 'That must be the bastard that got the drop on me! Tall guy with black hair and a fancy moustache?'

'That's the one.' Carney nodded.

'And you say he's working for Ned Wilkes?'

'That he is.'

Leapman smiled horribly. 'I think I'll pay him a visit. See how he likes it when I take him by surprise.'

'Not now,' Bobby-Jo interrupted impatiently. 'We've got more important business.'

'Hell,' Leapman began then he saw the look on his friend's face. And he realized that if they didn't help the Old Man he would be in almost as much trouble with him as Bobby-Jo. 'OK,' he said. 'I'll sort the bastard out later on.'

'And Charley and me'll help,' Bobby-Jo promised. 'Thing is, Jake, if this gambler rode into town with Kirkpatrick's gal . . .'

'Her name's Dowling.'

'Yeah, OK!' Bobby-Jo shouted, not liking it when someone broke his concentration. He began again. 'If the pair of 'em rode here then what makes you think she was at Freeman's when Pa shot Mills? They needn't've been anywhere near the place.'

'But, Bobby-Jo, think.'

The young man frowned hard in an attempt to do so, but he didn't succeed. Leapman and Burchell didn't look any more enlightened. Carney sighed and realized he'd have to explain carefully.

'The gambler came here from who knows where and I agree he probably travelled by horse. But the Dowling gal is from the East, like Kirkpatrick. She couldn't possibly have ridden all that way. It's too far.'

'Guess not.' Bobby-Jo had no real idea how far away the 'East' was but he supposed it must be farther than Mexico. 'So?'

'She must have travelled out here by the railroad. And she probably got off the train at Lordsburg, where she would've caught the Wells Fargo stage to Nogales. That'd be the quickest way. And if so she'd then change stagecoaches at Freeman's, wouldn't she? The stage was late leaving Felicidad that day. Quite likely she was there, waiting for it, when your pa caught up with Mills.'

'Yeah, she could've been,' Bobby-Jo said, voice rising with excitement. 'She must be the damn witness.' He looked round in triumph.

'Hold on, Bobby-Jo.' Leapman put a hand on the young man's arm. 'Mebbe she is the one, I ain't saying otherwise, but we dunno that for sure.'

'I spoke to the stagecoach driver.' Carney played his trump card. 'He admitted that on the way to Freeman's he and the guard met two riders – a man and a woman – and the man more or less said that the woman had been at the stage station and seen the bodies. Not only that but the man called her Miss Dowling and like I said Miss Dowling is the name of Kirkpatrick's fiancée!'

'Hell!' Bobby-Jo said. 'It is her, Larry. Who else could it be?' He breathed a silent sigh of relief. Finding the witness would surely be a way to please his father, get in his good books for once.

'It surely won't be difficult to find out,' Carney went on. He was pleased he'd been of use to the Hennesseys. It should stand him in good stead in the future.

Leapman grinned. 'That it won't. If we question

99

her she won't be able to resist telling us the truth.
Wonder where she is now?'

'That won't be difficult to find out neither,' Bobby-
Jo said.

'Stop her,' Carney said, 'and you stop the trial.'

Outside Lizzie stepped back from the window,
appalled. Didn't Carney realize he'd as good as
signed a young woman's death warrant? That even if
Miss Dowling wasn't the witness, Bobby-Jo could
hardly leave her alive after he and the others had
'questioned' her. Lizzie shivered, hardly daring to
imagine what form that questioning would take.

Didn't Carney care? Lizzie shook her head, thinking that, no, he probably didn't. All he ever cared
about was his own hide.

What should she do? What was there that she
could do?

Caring about her own safety, she was in enough
trouble as it was, Lizzie's first thought was to keep
quiet. Pretend she hadn't overheard the conversation. Then she knew that was impossible.

Marshal Kirkpatrick had always been kind to her.
Treated her fairly. Tried to help her. She couldn't let
his girlfriend, the girl he loved and hoped to marry,
be killed in order to save a thug like Bernie
Hennessey from the hangman. Lizzie knew no man
had ever loved her in that way, and never would,
wouldn't want to marry her, but she was a romantic
at heart and she often imagined what being loved by
a nice man and married to him would be like.

However scared she was she would have to warn

Kirkpatrick, warn them both.

Besides, she smiled, this might be her one and only chance to get her own back; not only on Carney but on the Hennesseys as well.

She opened the gate in the wall of the yard and let herself out into the alley. For once she would be brave and do what was right.

CHAPTER THIRTEEN

She should also warn that nice, handsome Mr Pitt.
Lizzie left the alley coming out by the side of The
Silver Dollar. She peered round the corner, making
sure Bobby-Jo and the others weren't heading this
way. They were probably enjoying a few more
whiskies in the hope that Carney wouldn't make
them pay. She pushed open the swing doors and
quickly stepped inside the saloon. At this hour of the
afternoon, the place was quiet, just one or two men
bellying up to the bar and, there, thank God, in the
corner, sitting by the roulette wheel, was Pitt.

'Hey, you!' Wilkes saw her and called to her
angrily. 'Out!'

Lizzie took no notice of him or of the curious
looks of the other men. She hurried over to Pitt.

'What's the matter?' he asked, getting to his feet.
He signalled to Wilkes that it was all right, Lizzie
wouldn't cause any trouble.

'Carney has told Larry, Hennessey's foreman, who
you are.' Lizzie caught hold of his hand. 'Larry don't
know your name but he knows where you work. He's

going to come here and get you for what you did to him.'

'I can handle Leapman,' Pitt said. 'But thanks for the warning.'

'You might be able to beat him if he was on his own but I know Larry and he won't be alone. He'll have Bobby-Jo and Charley Burchell to back him up.'

'I don't want any fighting or shooting in here,' Wilkes said from the bar. He couldn't hear all that Lizzie was saying but he knew from her face that it was something serious. And he'd heard the dreaded word: Hennessey.

'It's OK,' Pitt said.

'No, Mr Pitt, it ain't OK because that ain't all. Carney also told them that Marshal Kirkpatrick's girl-friend is the one willing to speak up about Bernie.'

'Oh, hell!'

'It's true then?'

'Yeah.' Pitt took Lizzie by the arm and gave her a gentle shake. 'How do you know all this?'

'I listened to them from outside.'

'What else did they say?'

'What do you think? They know if they get rid of her there'll be no trial.'

Pitt swore. 'We must tell them.'

'That's what I was on my way to do.'

'Ned, I've got to go out for a while,' Pitt said. He put on his hat and eased his gun in its holster.

'Where you going?' Wilkes asked. 'How long will you be?'

'Don't know. I'll be as quick as I can. Come on, Lizzie, let's go.'

'To the jailhouse?'

'Yeah. Kirkpatrick is probably there.'

But he wasn't. Instead Dave Vaughan was alone, sitting at his desk, shotgun within easy reach.

Vaughan said, 'Marshal Kirkpatrick thought that as it was quiet for the moment, and seeing as he didn't think he'd get another chance while the Hennesseys are in town, he'd go and visit Miss Dowling. Tell her what was happening. He hasn't been gone long. He'll soon be back.'

'This can't wait.'

'Then I expect he'll still be at the boarding house.'

'I can't go there,' Lizzie mumbled, dragging her heels. 'It's respectable! Mrs Barron don't approve of the likes of me.'

'I'll be with you,' Pitt said, taking hold of her hand.

'Can't you go and fetch the marshal, bring him back here?'

'No, there's no time.'

When they reached the boarding house it was obvious from Mrs Barron's face that she most certainly didn't approve of Lizzie. She looked as if she didn't particularly approve of Pitt either.

'The marshal and Miss Dowling are in the parlour,' she said in a very icy tone. 'I'm not sure . . .'

'I'm sorry, ma'am,' Pitt said, pushing by her. 'It's an emergency. We need to see them both. Where is it?'

With pursed lips Mrs Barron pointed to a door at the end of the hall.

Lizzie kept her eyes lowered as she followed Pitt,

feeling most uncomfortable in such surroundings and with Mrs Barron's eyes boring into her back. She wasn't made to feel any better when they went into the parlour and Thora's eyes widened. The girl also clearly recognized Lizzie for what she was and didn't appear to approve of her any more than Mrs Barron did.

Kirkpatrick and Thora were sitting together on a sofa, holding hands. They sprang apart and Kirkpatrick stood up.

'Pitt, what is it?'

'Lizzie has come from Carney's with something to say,' Pitt said. He too recognized Thora's disapproval and added, 'She's been very brave. Go on, Lizzie, tell them what you told me.'

Lizzie swallowed nervously. 'Marshal, miss. Oh, miss, Jake Carney told Bobby-Jo all about you. They all know you're the marshal's witness.'

While Thora turned white and her hands went to her mouth as if to stop herself from crying out, Kirkpatrick took a step towards Lizzie.

'Are you telling the truth?' he demanded, wondering if perhaps this was a trick on Carney's part.

Lizzie nodded and retreated behind Pitt.

'What are we going to do?' Thora said, getting up to stand by Kirkpatrick's side. She clutched at his arm. 'They'll mean me harm, won't they?'

'They know that without you I won't have a case against Hennessey,' Kirkpatrick admitted. 'Hell, I should never have agreed to let you testify.'

'It's too late for that,' Pitt said. 'They'll never believe Miss Dowling has changed her mind.'

105

'That's right,' Lizzie added. 'I know them. They won't take any chances. You must do something, marshal. I left as quick as I could but I don't know how far behind me they are.' She glanced at the parlour door as if expecting it to come crashing open and Bobby-Jo and Carney to be outside.

'Don't worry, I won't let anything happen to you.' Kirkpatrick put his arm around Thora, drawing her close.

'You can't keep Miss Dowling safe and guard Hennessey at the same time,' Pitt pointed out.

'I don't intend to.'

'You can't let Hennessey go,' Thora objected immediately. 'Not after all he's done. I won't let you.'

'I don't intend to do that either. Thora, sweetheart, I must get you out of town and hidden somewhere safe until Judge Corbett gets here and you're needed to give your testimony. It'll only be for a few days.'

'But I can't . . . where would I go?'

'Let me think.'

'What about me?' Lizzie asked in a small voice.

Kirkpatrick looked at the girl as if he'd forgotten she was in the room. 'You'll have to go back to Carney's.'

'Oh, Ralph, she might be in danger there,' Thora said. 'You can't send her back.'

'Does anyone know you were listening? That you've left the saloon?'

Lizzie shook her head.

'I don't like this,' Pitt said.

'I'll be all right.' Lizzie spoke more firmly than she felt.

'Are you sure?'

'Yeah, Mr Pitt. I'll be on my way before anyone misses me.'

'Lizzie.' Thora stopped the girl as she went to the door. She was ashamed of her earlier reaction and wanted to try to make amends. 'Thank you.'

Lizzie gave her a little smile before she left the room.

'She won't be hurt, will she?' Thora said, worry in her voice.

'Not if I can help it.'

'Where can Miss Dowling go she'll be safe?' Pitt asked. 'Ferguson's ranch?'

Kirkpatrick frowned. 'Normally that would be a good idea but not with nearly all his men out on spring round-up. And it's too close to the Hennesseys' place for my liking.'

'Where then?'

Kirkpatrick thought for a moment or two then smiled.

'Thora, there's a farm up in the hills. Owned by Fred and Ruth Walker. They're a real nice couple. I'm sure they'll hide you. And before he became a farmer Fred was a sergeant in the army; he doesn't stand any nonsense from anyone. It's not far but far enough the Hennesseys will never think of looking for you there. Why should they? We'll go directly when you've packed your bag with a few essentials.'

'But, Ralph, you can't take me. Your place is here. Making certain that Hennessey remains in jail and is ready to stand trial. Especially with his family in town. If they know you've left Felicidad they'll believe you're running away and there'll be nothing to stop them attacking the jail. There's Lizzie to think of as well. You must protect her.'

'My first concern is you. And you can't go on your own.'

'I'll take her,' Pitt said.

'You?' Kirkpatrick looked at the man uncertainly. 'I can't ask you to do that.'

'You ain't asking, I'm offering. Think about it. It's the only possible solution.'

'You'll take Thora, Miss Dowling, to the farm and then come back?'

'Of course. You can trust me.'

'I'll be all right with Mr Pitt,' Thora added, smiling at the other man.

Still looking a bit doubtful, but knowing he had no choice – Thora needed to be got out of Felicidad as soon as possible – Kirkpatrick turned to the girl. 'If you leave right now, you should get to the farm by nightfall. You go and pack while I give Pitt directions.'

An anxious Mrs Barron was waiting on the other side of the door.

'Thora, my dear, is everything all right? What's going on?'

'I have to leave Felicidad for a short while,' Thora said. 'It seems the Hennesseys have found out who I am and what I saw.'

'Oh no!'

'Don't worry.' Thora gave the woman a quick hug. 'I shall be back soon.'

Hoping she was right, Thora ran up to her room. More horse riding! She was only just recovering from the ride from the stage station to Felicidad and now she had another long ride in front of her. Her arrival here was just going from bad to worse.

CHAPTER FOURTEEN

'Pitt, are you sure about this?' Kirkpatrick asked once Thora had gone. 'You really don't mind?'

'No, I don't mind.' And Pitt didn't because he felt he had no choice. But he couldn't help but wonder exactly how he'd become caught up in all this, especially as it wasn't anything to do with him.

'And you'll come straight back once you've delivered Thora to the Walkers?'

'Yeah, don't worry, Miss Dowling and her reputation will be safe with me. I'm a gambler. I belong with girls like Lizzie not decent young ladies like your Thora.'

Kirkpatrick reddened. 'I didn't mean ... that is ...'

'And I'll be safe with Miss Dowling,' Pitt added with a grin to show he took no offence. 'She loves you, very much.' He paused. 'Talking of Lizzie, you'll look out for her, won't you? You owe her.'

'I know that. I'll do my best. Hopefully no one will find out she's been here to warn me. God, what a mess this is. I hope when it's over Thora doesn't decide New Mexico is too dangerous and want to go back to Pennsylvania. I couldn't blame her if she did.'

'I'm sure she won't.'

Kirkpatrick turned as the door opened. 'Ah, here she is. Have you got all you need? Are you ready to leave?'

Thora nodded. She tried to smile, determined not to let Ralph know how scared she was.

'We'd better get started,' Pitt said, taking hold of Thora's bag.

'If I know anything about Bobby-Jo and the others they'll still be at Carney's, drinking their way through a bottle of whiskey,' Kirkpatrick said on the way to the livery stable. 'By the time they've finished you'll be well on your way and they'll have no way of knowing where you've gone or in which direction. And the first part of the trail to the farm is fairly well travelled by other farmers and ranchers so they won't be able to pick up your tracks.'

'I'm sorry, Mrs Burchell, but I can't sell you any more whiskey.'

Mr Toombs was a short and thin man and Belle towered over him but he stood his ground.

'What d'you mean?' Belle asked harshly. 'I can clearly see several bottles of whiskey up there on that shelf. Do you see them too?' she added sarcastically.

'Yeah I know they're there.'

'Well then? Get them for me you stupid little man.'

One of the other customers tutted at Belle's rudeness. Belle swung round to glare at the woman who

111

to Belle's surprise took no notice.

'I'm not giving you or your family any more credit, Mrs Burchell. Pay me what you owe and I'll sell you more goods. But not until then.'

All the other customers clapped.

Belle didn't know what to say or do. The Hennesseys rarely handed money over for anything and no one had ever dared demand payment. Until now. She leant her hands on the counter and thrust her body forward threateningly.

'You're only being like this because Pa is in jail . . .'

'Best place for him,' someone said.

'. . . You wait until he gets out! He'll show you, show all of you, what it means to be rude to a Hennessey!' She pointed a finger at Toombs, 'And don't forget Bobby-Jo is still free. He'll deal with you later.'

Toombs didn't look particularly scared of that threat. Probably because he knew as well as everyone else that when Bobby-Jo was in town without his father to keep an eye on him he spent the time drinking until he was too drunk to do anything but sleep it off.

'Get out of my place now,' he said.

'Yes, go on, your kind aren't welcome in decent places.'

Belle marched out of the store, deliberately knocking over a display of canned fruit as she did so.

She wanted to get Bobby-Jo and Larry and teach these idiots a real hard lesson. But she knew that that would have to wait until they'd freed the Old Man. She stopped suddenly. There was the marshal with two companions on the other side of the plaza. Frowning, she quickly stepped back into the shadows cast by the store overhang. Something was going on. She recognized the man with Kirkpatrick. Who was the girl? Belle hadn't seen her before. Why did Kirkpatrick look so concerned? He had his arm round the girl and was hurrying her along. Where were they going?

Of all the Hennesseys, Belle was the only one with any brains. She came to the conclusion that perhaps this girl was the person her father thought was out at Freeman's stage station. The witness who was the reason for his arrest!

Belle decided to follow them, discover where they were going, see if she was wrong or right. They turned into the stables. Then she was certain. Kirkpatrick was getting his witness out of town, was going to hide her somewhere. He mustn't succeed.

Where was Bobby-Jo when she needed him? Belle bet he was still down at Carney's, not even bothering about their father. She turned round and broke into a run. Her brother needed to learn about this. Needed to do something. Hopefully he and the others wouldn't already be drunk and incapable.

'It won't be for long.' Kirkpatrick took Thora into his arms, giving her a reassuring squeeze. 'And you'll be free from danger at the farm.'

'Don't worry about me, Ralph, just make sure everything is all right here.'

'I will. I'll see you soon. I'll come for you once the judge arrives. Look after her, Pitt.'

Kirkpatrick helped Thora into the saddle and walked to the door, watching as Pitt and Thora rode away. At the corner, Thora looked back and waved and then she was gone. He sighed heavily. If only this whole damn business was finished with. The damn Hennesseys!

Speaking of who . . . he decided that as soon as he'd checked in with Dave Vaughan and made sure all was secure at the jailhouse, he'd better go down to the redlight district and find out what Bobby-Jo and his cohorts were up to.

When Belle reached Carney's, she was thankful to find her brother and her husband, and Leapman, were still there, drinking. At least they hadn't moved on to the brothel and at least they were still standing up. She hurried over to them and shook Bobby-Jo until he took notice of her. She quickly told them what she'd seen.

'Hell,' Bobby-Jo said with a glance at Carney. 'It must be that girl you told us about.'

'What I'd like to know is why Kirkpatrick is getting her out of town all of a sudden?' Leapman said.

'Could he've somehow found out we knew about her?' Bobby-Jo said.

'Mebbe, but how?'

'How indeed?' Carney glanced around the room. Who might have overheard their conversation and seen fit to warn the marshal? Who would dare?

'For God's sake shut up! It doesn't matter how he knows!' Belle screeched, pummelling at Bobby-Jo's chest. 'All the while you're talking the more likely it is she'll get away. We've gotta go after her while we can.'

Kirkpatrick was surprised when he walked into Carney's and saw no sign of any of the Hennessey clan. Aware of the few customers warily watching him, one or two getting up to leave, he strode up to the bar.

'Well, hello there, Marshal, what can I do for you?' Carney asked with a smirk. 'Or has someone been complaining 'bout me again? When as usual I ain't done nothing. Or are you here just to frighten away my customers?'

'Where's Hennessey and his friends?'

'Hennessey? Thought he was in jail.'

'I haven't got time to play games.' Kirkpatrick clenched his hands into fists.

'Oh.' Carney gave another smirk. 'You mean Bobby-Jo?' He looked round in an exaggerated manner. 'Umm, sorry, Marshal, I don't see him.'

'He has been here though?'

'Yeah. Guess so.'

'When did he leave?'

'Umm, I'm not certain. A short while ago I guess.'

'Where was he going?'

'That I don't know.'

'You don't know anything much, do you, Jake?'

'Nothing that would help you, no.'

Keeping a grip on his temper, Kirkpatrick left the saloon, aware of laughter breaking out behind him. He promised himself that one of these days he'd not only shut Carney's down but give Carney something to think about that he wouldn't find in the least bit funny. As he walked along the sidewalk he tried not to worry. Bobby-Jo and the others must have moved on to Price's brothel. There was no way they could have gone after Thora and Pitt.

Following the directions Kirkpatrick had given him, Pitt found the way to the Walkers' farm quickly took them up into the hills, the mountains looming, slopes pine-clad and rocky, close by. They rode in the opposite direction to the Hennessey ranch, along what was at first a fairly wide track so that he thought they should make good time. Even so, although Kirkpatrick might not like it, he would probably have to stay the night at the farm. He couldn't risk his horse, or himself, trying to find his way back to Felicidad in the dark. He hoped Ned Wilkes would understand and that he still had a job dealing poker at The Silver Dollar. He certainly hadn't spent much time there so far.

He didn't know what to say to Thora. She was obviously very frightened, obviously missing Ralph, worrying about him even while Ralph was worrying about her. Perhaps both were regretting their decision to come West to seek their fortune.

But after a while she rode up beside him and broke the silence.

'This is beautiful country, isn't it?' She raised her face to the sun. 'Is it good farming country?'

'It looks like it to me,' Pitt said, although the farm he'd grown up on had been in the flat treeless plains of the mid-West. 'Good for cattle as well. The animals

116

can be driven up here when it becomes hot and the lower slopes lose their grass. Ah, we turn here.'

They had come to a fork in the trail. One way led higher into the hills, the other turned left and sloped away across a wide valley.

'I don't think it's much further.'

Thora didn't ask how far that might be. She had found that distances out West were different to back home in Pennsylvania and that Pitt's idea of not much further was probably quite different to hers. Instead she gritted her teeth and tried not to mind too much the bumping up and down of the horse.

After a while she glanced at Pitt. He'd turned in his saddle more than once since they started across the valley as if he was looking back at something. He was frowning. And now he stopped his horse.

'What's the matter?' she asked, her heart beginning to thud.

Pitt didn't want to worry Thora but at the same time he didn't see the point in keeping things from her.

'We're being followed,' he said.

CHAPTER FIFTEEN

'Oh!' Thora gave a little gasp. 'Are you sure?'

'I'm sure we're being followed,' Pitt said. 'But not who by.' He turned in the saddle to point along their back trail. 'There's someone's dust, d'you see?'

Thora nodded. 'Can you tell who it is?'

'No, but whoever it is has been coming after us slowly and steadily for a while now. They're still some way away but they're catching up.'

'Who could it be but the Hennesseys?'

'There are ranches and farms in these hills and this track is well travelled. And I don't see how they could have known we left town, but . . .'

'But you think it's them, don't you?'

'Yeah, I'm afraid I do. We daren't take a chance on thinking otherwise.'

'So what should we do? Make a dash for it?'

Thora hoped Pitt wouldn't agree to that suggestion. She wasn't a good enough horsewoman to ride fast, especially in such uncertain terrain, for a long distance. To her relief he shook his head.

'That ain't the answer. We'd raise up so much dust that it'd be visible for miles, all they'd have to do is follow it. And it ain't any use continuing on this way either.'

'Why not? The idea is to get to the Walkers' farm isn't it?'

'Yeah but we don't want to lead the Hennesseys right there.'

'No, of course not. What then?'

Knowing all the while they remained where they were the nearer their pursuers came, Pitt quickly made up his mind.

'Let's ride back to that turn off and take the other fork leading away from the farm. Once we get higher in the hills we'll ride across country. That way we'll soon find out if whoever it is is still after us.'

'What if they are?'

'We'll have to try to lose them. There should be plenty of opportunities to hide our tracks. And then we can wait somewhere until they give up.'

Pitt made it sound easy but Thora had the feeling it wasn't going to be quite as easy as he said. As she pulled on the reins to guide her horse after his, she said, 'I wonder if Ralph has realized the Hennesseys have come after us.'

'If he has there's nothing he can do about it,' Pitt told her. 'We're on our own.'

Kirkpatrick was, in fact, beginning to suspect that Bobby-Jo had somehow found out that Thora had left Felicidad and he and the others had ridden after

119

her. There was no sign of any of the clan around the Redlight District. No one had seen them. Even Belle had disappeared. He couldn't imagine them just returning to their ranch. Stomach churning with fear, feeling sick, he cursed having sent Thora away, cursed not having gone with her. If anything happened to her . . .

He debated whether or not to ride after her but he knew that if the Hennesseys were following her by the time he caught up he'd be too late to help. It would all be over. All he could do was trust in Pitt to handle the situation while he waited in town and guarded Old Man Hennessey. Waiting! He'd never been any good at waiting and doing nothing.

Hoping against hope he was wrong he decided to go back to Carney's. Maybe Bobby-Jo and the other two had decided to enjoy the girls who worked there rather than go down to the brothel. In the circumstances Jake Carney might have wanted to keep in their good books by offering the girls' services for free. It would be just like him not to tell Kirkpatrick but let him go off on a wild goose chase.

Once the saloon had quietened down after the marshal's visit, Carney left one of his more reliable customers, a man who wore a patch over his left eye and so was imaginatively nick-named One-Eye, in charge of the bar. He went through the door into the rear.

'Lizzie!' he yelled.

The girl opened her bedroom door. She looked

frightened but that didn't necessarily mean anything. Every girl he'd ever employed was always frightened of him. It was how Carney kept control.

'Yeah, Jake?'

'Where you been?'

'I didn't feel well. I was lying down. I'll be ready for this evening I promise.'

'You were in the bar earlier.' Carney stood in front of her, hands on his hips.

'Yeah and then I didn't feel well.'

'You didn't ask my permission to leave, did you?'

'You was busy. I'm sorry.' Lizzie lowered her eyes but not before he'd seen the fear flare in them.

'I missed you 'bout the time Bobby-Jo came in.'

'That right? I didn't see him.' Lizzie gulped nervously and hoped she sounded convincing.

'No? Now why don't I believe you?'

'It's the truth.'

'I suppose you didn't happen to listen in to our conversation and then run off and tell Kirkpatrick what you overheard?'

'Overheard? No, Jake, I wouldn't listen to anything I shouldn't.' Lizzie's heart sank. She might have known Carney would work out what had happened. What would he do to her? 'And I'd never repeat anything to Kirkpatrick. Why should I?' She gave a little laugh. 'I don't like him no more'n you do.'

'Somehow I don't believe that either. It could only've been you.' Carney's hand shot out and slapped Lizzie round her face.

She cried out in shock and pain and slumped back

121

against the wall.

'No, Jake, please, don't. I'm telling you the truth. I wouldn't do nothing to hurt you, nor the Hennesseys, you know that.'

'We'll see 'bout that won't we?' And Carney began to undo his belt. 'Bout time you had a good whipping. Causing me no end of trouble like you have. Get in there.' He caught her arm spinning her into the bedroom.

'Jake, no, please, please,' Lizzie whimpered. It was useless to beg but she knew her punishment would be even worse if she didn't.

'Shut up,' Carney said and kicked the door shut.

'Back again, Marshal?' One-Eye said as Kirkpatrick came into the saloon. 'What do we owe this pleasure to?'

'Where's Carney?'

'Don't rightly know.' Obviously his customers weren't any more helpful than Carney. 'He had business out back. And, Marshal, no you can't go on back there. It's private.'

'Well, you just tell . . .' Kirkpatrick began.

And stopped as a scream came from somewhere behind the door. Screams weren't unusual in Carney's, especially at night, but this was late afternoon and it sounded as if someone was terrified and in awful pain.

'Christ!' Kirkpatrick's heart twisted.

'It ain't your business,' One-Eye said.

Lizzie; was it Lizzie in trouble?

'I'm making it my business.' He shoved the man

aside. He was going to stop this. Should have stopped it a long while ago.

'You can't . . .'

Kirkpatrick took no notice. He was through the door before One-Eye could stop him, slamming it shut in the man's face. He found himself in a short and dirty corridor with an open door leading to the yard on one side and three more doors leading to bedrooms.

Another scream.

One of Carney's other girls, Kirkpatrick knew her name was Marlene, stood in the hall. She had tears in her eyes and as she saw the lawman she pointed to the door opposite.

'Is it Lizzie?'

Marlene nodded.

Kirkpatrick kicked the door open.

Carney stood in the middle of the room, arm raised high, belt in his hand. Lizzie lay at his feet. Her clothes were torn and blood covered her arms and back. Even as Kirkpatrick yelled at him to stop, Carney brought the belt down hard on Lizzie's back. The girl screamed and then moaned.

'You bastard,' Kirkpatrick snarled. 'Leave her alone.'

'Keep out of it.' Carney swirled round. He swung the belt, trying to hit Kirkpatrick with it.

Kirkpatrick ducked, feeling the whoosh of the buckle by his ear. Quickly he stepped forward and punched the man on the jaw as hard as he could. Carney staggered, tripped and fell onto the bed.

'Lizzie, are you . . .'

'Marshal, look out!'

Kirkpatrick looked up. Carney had pulled a hide-out gun from his trouser leg. He was aiming it. Kirkpatrick cursed his stupidity. He'd thought Carney was unarmed but he should have known the man would keep a gun on him. He drew his own gun . . . he would be too late. Carney was ready to shoot. He couldn't miss at this distance.

Somehow Lizzie raised herself from the floor and jogged Carney's arm even as he fired. The bullet went wide, slamming into the wall behind the marshal. It was his only shot.

Kirkpatrick had the drop on Carney now. He could arrest him. Then he thought of the way the man had ill-treated Lizzie. How he'd betrayed Thora.

'No.' Carney's ever present smirk changed to one of terror as he saw the look in the marshal's eyes. 'No, don't,' he cried.

'You bastard,' Kirkpatrick said. And he pulled the trigger, twice.

Both bullets struck Carney in the chest. With a gasp he dropped his gun and collapsed back on the bed. He groaned once and then was silent.

'Lizzie.' Kirkpatrick went over to the girl, who had fallen back on the floor. She was weeping and moaning with pain.

'He knew I told you. He was so mad I thought he'd kill me.'

'I know, I know, but it's all right now. He can't hurt you ever again.' Gently Kirkpatrick put his arms round the girl and eased her to her feet. She collapsed against him. 'Come on, I'm getting you out of here.'

He looked up and saw Marlene and another girl standing in the doorway, arms round one another, several of the customers peering over their shoulders.

'You can leave as well,' he told the two girls. 'Carney can't hurt you either.'

'You shot him when he was surrendering,' One-Eye accused. 'I done see you.'

'It didn't look that way to me,' Marlene said and the other girl nodded in agreement. 'Looked to me like Carney didn't give Marshal Kirkpatrick no choice.'

'Leave it alone, all of you,' Kirkpatrick said. 'No one in their right minds would think me guilty after what he was and what he's done.'

He didn't need to say any more as he lifted the now unconscious Lizzie up into his arms. Everyone backed away. Kirkpatrick wondered if he ought to feel guilty over shooting Carney but he didn't. The man had it coming. If anything he felt good.

'Where you taking her?' Marlene asked.

'To Mrs Barron's boarding house.'

'She don't approve of whores.'

'She won't turn away a girl who's been hurt like Lizzie has just for trying to help me.'

'Will she be all right?' Marlene reached over to push a lock of Lizzie's hair out of the girl's eyes.

'I surely hope so.'

'By the way, Marshal.' Marlene caught at Kirkpatrick's arm. 'It was that bitch, Belle, told

Bobby-Jo 'bout your witness leaving town. I seen 'em ride out directly.'

Thora, Kirkpatrick thought with sinking heart, what was happening to Thora? He'd saved Lizzie. What if he couldn't save Thora?

CHAPTER SIXTEEN

Pitt knew it was pointless to remain on the dirt trail. They had to find a place to hide, or at least somewhere he could hide their tracks. So once they were beyond a stand of cottonwoods, he turned away into open country.

He and Thora rode through high grass, in and out of piñon trees and by spindly juniper bushes. Ever climbing, passing outcrops of jagged rocks, the ground becoming broken and the air cooler. After a while they found themselves nearly at the edge of the forests of ponderosa pine that covered the first slopes of the mountains.

'Are they still behind us?' Thora asked when Pitt paused for a few moments to look back.

'I can't see anyone,' he said. 'But that doesn't mean they ain't coming. There's not much shelter here so let's go on a bit farther, find out what's over the next rise.'

Pitt was extremely worried, although he hoped Thora didn't realize. He wanted to make sure they had given the Hennesseys the slip, which he feared they hadn't, but he didn't want to go so far out of their way they became lost. Neither did he want to find himself and Thora in the mountains when night fell and it would quickly become very cold. And time was ebbing away. Already deep shadows were forming along the slopes.

Thora nodded reluctantly. 'All right.' Her whole body ached, pains shooting up and down her spine and she wondered if she would be able to walk when she came to dismount. She decided she mustn't complain when Pitt was doing his best for her and needn't be doing anything at all.

Reaching the top of the rise and coming out of the trees they found themselves at the bottom of another hill where a fast running stream cascaded down the steep slope, before spilling away out of sight amongst the pine-trees. At the top of the hill was a line of rocks and tall boulders.

'We'll climb up there,' Pitt decided.

Thora looked doubtful.

'There's nowhere else we can go,' Pitt said. 'Don't worry, it looks as if there's a fairly easy way up by the side of the stream. And once we reach the top the rocks will give us a safe place to rest for a while and also be a good vantage point from where we can look all round without being spotted.'

They might find out where they were too.

'We're catching up!' Leapman said, with a grin.

He dismounted to study the ground, his sharp eyes seeing where two horses had passed recently. He was a good tracker and although Pitt had done his best to hide their trail his best wasn't good enough to deceive Leapman.

'Are you sure it's them?' Burchell asked, not for the first time. He wanted to be back in Felicidad, drinking and gambling, not riding round the lower slopes of the Mimbres Mountains, when it was getting dark and cold.

'Of course it's them,' Belle said crossly. 'Who else could it be? We followed 'em from town and after a while they began to criss-cross the country obviously trying to escape us. Who else would do that?'

Burchell thought a great number of people might go out of their way to escape the Hennesseys.

'Don't keep making difficulties. If you don't want to help you can go back to the ranch.'

Belle's tone of voice dared Burchell to do so.

Bobby-Jo was getting fed up with their bickering. He jigged his horse up close to Leapman. 'How far in front are they?'

'Not far. One of 'em, the gal I guess, ain't much of a rider. She's slowing the other one up.'

Belle rode out of the trees. She shrieked. 'There they are!' She pointed to the next slope up which two riders were slowly making their way, with some difficulty by the looks of things. 'C'mon! We've got 'em!' She turned to her brother her eyes shining. 'We can tell Kirkpatrick he ain't no longer got a witness and he'll have to set Pa free.'

It didn't take Pitt long to realize he'd made a mistake. The way up by the stream might have looked easy from below but it certainly wasn't. It was almost sheer, the more so the higher they climbed, the ground was muddy and slippery, with hidden stones. The horses slid more than they climbed. They should have followed the stream down the hill, not up. But it was too late to go back now. They had to reach the top. It was their only chance.

He heard Thora give a little cry. He glanced back. She could hardly manage her animal.

'Get off your horse,' he called to her. 'We'll lead them. Here, give me the reins, I'll handle both horses while you see to yourself.'

'You won't be able to.'

'Yeah, I will. Go on.'

Thora passed him by, almost on her hands and knees, scrabbling at the ground for support. At the same moment something whined by them and landed in the stream, sending up a little spout of water. Even as Thora looked in that direction, wondering what it was, they both heard the retort of a rifle. The Hennesseys had caught up.

'Get down!' Pitt said and shoved at Thora's back.

She fell to the ground and lay there, tired and terrified.

'What shall we do?' she asked. 'Can we get to the top?'

'We've got to.'

Pitt looked up the slope. The rocks still seemed a long way away and in between there was little or no cover. He stared back. Their pursuers – four of them – were at the bottom of the hill. Getting ready to come after them. But, he thought, they would find it just as hard to climb the slope as he and Thora had done.

Then he saw the Hennesseys had learned from Pitt's mistake. They had already dismounted, were leaving the horses behind, would climb more quickly without them, and one of the men, the one with the rifle, had taken up a position from which to shoot at him and Thora. They would make clear targets if they made a move but neither could they stay put and wait for their pursuers to catch up.

Quickly he pulled his rifle from its scabbard. He let go of the horses, they would have to see to themselves; to his relief they headed for the top of the hill. He crouched down by Thora and handed her his pistol.

'Can you shoot?'

'No, of course I can't,' Thora said rather indignantly, dismay in her eyes.

'Well, try. You just aim the gun and pull the trigger.'

'I don't think I can. Supposing I kill someone?'

'That's the idea,' Pitt told her grimly. 'Don't forget, they're trying to kill us. Let's go. Try to keep low. You can do it. Don't give up, not now.'

Together, helping one another, pushing and shoving and tugging, they inched their way up the slope, through the cloying mud. They were followed by shots from the rifle below. Whoever was doing the firing wasn't much of a shot. None of the bullets came close. Pitt had a terrible feeling in the pit of his stomach that maybe the shooter was toying with them. Would allow them to almost reach the rocks and believe they were safe, and would then prove he was a good shot after all.

But each step took them further away from the rifle's range and he began to permit himself a little hope. They were almost at the top. Reach the rocks, climb over and they would be in a good position.

A shot came from up close.

Thora screamed.

'You hit?'

'No, surprised that's all. And there's mud in my eye. I can't see properly.'

Another shot.

Pitt rolled over on to his back.

'Shit,' he muttered.

Bobby-Jo and Burchell weren't far below them, half hidden by a couple of boulders. He raised his rifle and sent several bullets in their direction. Their two guns opened up on him. And where was Belle? He couldn't see her anywhere. But there had been four riders. She must still be at the bottom with Leapman.

'Go on,' Pitt ordered Thora, who lay on the ground, trembling. 'Keep down.'

Again Thora began to crawl through the mud. It clung to her hands and feet, to her clothes, seeming to drag her back, making every move an exhausting effort. She was getting nowhere. She would never reach the top; instead she would die here face down in the mud. She hadn't gone very far when someone or something snared her foot. She screamed with fright and glanced over her shoulder.

It was Belle!

Belle must have climbed up the other side of the stream, where they hadn't seen her, and waded through the water. Grinning in triumph, she now tugged at Thora's ankle.

'Got you, you bitch!' she cried. She raised her gun.

Thora forgot all about Pitt's pistol. Instead she reacted instinctively and kicked out hard with the foot that was free. She caught Belle on the side of the head. Believing Thora presented an easy target Belle was taken by surprise. She let go of Thora's ankle. Thora kicked out again, with both feet this time, thudding them into the other girl's chest.

Belle's feet slipped in the mud. She found herself falling over the edge of the riverbank. She let go of the gun in an effort to grab at something, anything, to stop her fall. She almost succeeded in catching hold of a plant growing on the bank but Thora kicked her again as hard as she could.

Shoved backwards Belle's hands clutched air. Her face revealed her panic as she dropped back into the stream. The water was running too fast for her to gain any purchase and her feet gave way under her. She screamed. The force of the stream caught her; sending her tumbling down the hill, turning over and over again. She could do nothing to stop herself plummeting all the way to the bottom.

The shooting from below stopped as Leapman jumped in the water, ready to catch Belle.

As he saw what was happening, Burchell stood up. 'Belle!' he cried.

Pitt shot him.

'Go, go!' he yelled.

Thora hurried to obey. No more shots followed them. Somehow they reached the rocks, scrambled amongst them, over them, were on the far side. Safe.

Thora collapsed on the ground, gasping for breath, while Pitt fell on his knees beside her.

After a while he managed to summon up enough energy to look back down the way they'd come.

Burchell's body lay where it had fallen. Bobby-Jo had left him to slip and slide back down the hill to where Leapman had succeeded in pulling Belle out of the stream. The girl lay unmoving on the ground and Pitt didn't know if she was dead or not and right then he didn't care.

CHAPTER SEVENTEEN

'Belle! Belle, you OK?' Bobby-Jo yelled as he reached his sister and Leapman.

From where she sat on the ground the girl gave him a scathing glare. 'Apart from being soaked, freezing cold and bruised all over, yeah, Bobby-Jo, I'm fine.'

'What happened?'

'That bitch kicked me and I slipped in the mud.'

Belle hated having been got the better of, especially by another young woman and one from the East at that. She'd thought killing the girl would be oh so easy and she would be able to boast to her father that she was the one who'd got rid of the witness and saved him from jail. It hadn't worked out like that and she was furious. She was also recovering from the shock of her fall and the fear she would be killed, but she would never admit to any weakness to her brother.

'Did you shoot 'em both?'

'No.' Bobby-Jo shook his head.

'Why the hell not?'

'Charley was shot and then I saw you in the stream

falling down the hill. I decided to find out if you was OK.' It sounded a lame excuse even to Bobby-Jo and Belle wasn't fooled by it.

'You've never shown any concern 'bout me before, so why now? Oh, I know,' she spat out. 'You didn't want to face 'em by yourself. You damn coward!'

This was close enough to the truth that Bobby-Jo went red.

'They can't have gotten far. We can go after them,' he said trying to make amends.

'Don't be so damned stupid!' Belle screeched. 'If we climb the hill they can either wait to shoot us down or run off so by the time we get to the top they'll be long gone. And it's getting dark, Larry'll never track 'em. Will you?'

'Belle's right,' Leapman said. 'And we need to get her home so she can get out of those wet clothes.'

'Oh, thank you too for your concern.'

'Larry did save your life,' Bobby-Jo pointed out.

'He pulled me out of the damn stream that's all. Now shut up and help me.' When Belle was on her feet she stared back up the hill. 'Is Charley dead?'

'Yeah, I think so. He went down and didn't move.'

Belle scowled at Bobby-Jo and again he reddened; he hadn't stayed around to find out.

'We'd better go up and make sure.'

'No, leave him,' Belle said. 'He always was more damn trouble than he was worth.'

Leapman said, 'Bobby-Jo and me didn't like Charley much either but we can't just go off and leave him here. He might only be wounded. And if he's dead he needs to be buried or the vultures'll get him.'

'Oh, all right, I'll wait here while you two go and find out. What a fuss!' Belle crossed her arms over her chest. 'And hurry up, I'm cold.' She was also starting to ache all over.'

'Belle's right 'bout one thing,' Bobby-Jo said as he and Leapman started up the hill. 'Kirkpatrick's witness is free and clear. We don't know where she's goin'. And Pa is still in danger of being hanged. He ain't gonna be best pleased.'

Leapman thought about the situation for a few moments. 'All we can do is seize our chance to break your pa out of jail. '

'Hell, Larry, that way we risk getting hurt. I know Kirkpatrick is a damn greenhorn but anyone can pull the trigger on a shotgun. I don't fancy getting an ass-load of buckshot. There must be another way.'

'Well, I can't think of one, can you?'

Naturally Bobby-Jo couldn't.

'Look, I know we couldn't do anything today but that was because the marshal was expecting us. What if we wait till he ain't expecting us and attack the jail then? We shoot the bastard, the deputy will fade away. And if he doesn't he can be shot too.'

'Yeah, mebbe you're right,' Bobby-Jo said. He wasn't eager about the idea but they had to do something to rescue his father. Facing Old Man Hennessey's wrath if they didn't would prove worse than facing a shotgun!

'If we go in at night, no-one'll see us. We can take that bastard marshal by surprise. And afterwards I might've time to go and sort out that dealer at The Silver Dollar.'

Bobby-Jo was persuaded. 'OK. We'll tell Belle what we've decided. It'll have to be tomorrow now. And then, Larry, we ride for Mexico.'

'Yeah, Mexico.' Leapman wished they were there now.

When Mrs Barron came into the parlour, Kirkpatrick stood up, twisting his hat round in his hands.

'How's Lizzie?'

'She's very weak but with care she'll recover.' Mrs Barron shook her head. 'How one person can treat another in such a way I surely don't know. All I can say is it's a good thing you intervened when you did. The poor girl would have died otherwise. And I'm sure I speak for every decent person in town when I say it's even more of a good thing that Felicidad will no longer have to suffer an animal like Jake Carney in its midst.'

'I should have acted sooner.'

'Well, you've acted now.'

'Mrs Barron, can Lizzie stay here? Until she gets better that is.'

The woman nodded. She didn't approve of Lizzie and her kind but Kirkpatrick was right when he'd said she wouldn't turn away someone who needed her help.

'And when she is better?'

'I don't know. I imagine that if Old Man Hennessey is still around she'll leave Felicidad rather than become involved with him again.'

Fear flared in Mrs Barron's eyes. She knew as well as everyone else what it would mean for the town if

Hennessey was released from jail. He would be in a fine fury and he and his family would take it out on everyone.

'But he won't be around surely? At the very least the judge will sentence him to life imprisonment, won't he?'

'He will if Thora is . . .' Kirkpatrick gulped. 'That is if she's alive to testify against him. I'm so worried about her.' Tears came into his eyes.

Mrs Barron hurried over to the marshal and put a hand on his arm. 'Oh, she'll be all right, she must be. Oh, I surely hope and pray nothing bad happens to her.'

'So do I.'

With a heavy heart, Kirkpatrick left the boarding house, heading back for his office. It was almost dark now. The stores were closing for the night and nearly everyone had gone home. Perhaps when he reached the jailhouse Pitt would be there to tell him that he'd left Thora safe and well at the Walkers' farmhouse. But there was no sign of the man.

Was he being too hopeful in thinking Pitt should be back by now? Perhaps he would even decide to stay the night at the farm; it had been quite late when they set out. Or had something happened to them? Pitt was reliable but would he be a match for the Hennesseys, especially if he didn't realize until too late that they were on his trail? As for Thora, what would she do if faced with real danger? How would she cope when she had already been through so much?

When the door opened he looked up but hope

died when a small delegation of townspeople, led by Mr Toombs, came in.

'What can I do for you?' Kirkpatrick asked, hoping they weren't going to criticize him for shooting Jake Carney. He was thinking he'd hand over his badge if they did.

Toombs took off his hat and twisted it round in his hands. 'Marshal, we're here to offer you help all the while you've got Hennessey locked up.'

'Well, that's good of you,' Kirkpatrick said, trying not to sound surprised.

'It's not fair that you and your deputy should take all the risks and do all the work while we sit back and do nothing, when getting rid of the Hennesseys will benefit the whole town. Even if we don't actually help guard the jail we can help with some of your other work.'

'Thanks. I'll come up with some ideas and let you know.'

'Good. You're doing a splendid job, both you and your deputy. We just thought you should know that. Goodnight, Mr Kirkpatrick, Deputy.'

'That's a surprise,' Vaughan said, when they'd gone.

'Yes, I know.' Kirkpatrick paused. 'You know, Dave, everyone has always been scared of the Hennesseys, me included, but now I'm not so sure that there's anything special about them. We should have stood up against them a long time ago.'

'Well, it's happening now.'

A little while later Kirkpatrick went through to the cells to make sure Hennessey was secure for the

140

night. The man glared at him and muttered some threats but Kirkpatrick took no notice. Old Man Hennessey looked and sounded like an old man and neither he nor his threats had the power to frighten him. Back in his office he paced to the door to look out. Still no sign of Pitt.

'There's no point in worrying,' Vaughan said. 'Mebbe Pitt missed the way or something might've happened to one of the horses. There could be any number of reasons why he's not back yet and anyhow there ain't nothing you can do. You've just got to wait.'

'I know,' Kirkpatrick agreed. He sat down and ran a hand through his hair, forcing himself not to get up and go to the door again. 'But I can't help it.'

He wanted to worry about Thora without being told there was no point. Where the Hennesseys were concerned there was every point.

CHAPTER EIGHTEEN

Old Man Hennessey watched Kirkpatrick leave. Once he'd gone, Hennessey slumped down on his bunk. With his defiance gone, he was dispirited and afraid.

Why was he still locked up? Bobby-Jo and Belle had ridden into town to rescue him. Where were they? Why hadn't they broken him out? He couldn't believe that kids of his would let a damn Eastern greenhorn, and a fat deputy, get the better of them. That they'd run away. Well, they'd better hurry up and set him free or he'd give them hell! And as for that Lizzie . . . He loved her and she'd betrayed him. Hennessey brushed away tears of self-pity.

With nothing else to do he lay down and stared up at the dirty ceiling. He tried shutting his eyes but as he then saw a gallows and a noose, and crowds of people waiting to watch him die, he quickly opened them again. His face clouded over with fear. He must get out of here. He must.

He'd murdered three people and been seen doing it. There was no way Judge Corbett wouldn't decide that was a hanging offence. And, oh God, he didn't want to be hanged. He was afraid of dying and afraid that he would show himself up as a coward in front of those who would come to see the show.

Where were his kids? Where was help when he needed it?

When Pitt had recovered sufficiently to feel he could move again, even though he didn't want to, he heaved himself to his feet, his whole body protesting. He peered over the rocks, breathing a sigh of relief at what he saw. Their two horses were grazing not far away and he caught them up without any difficulty. Limping slightly he led them back to where Thora still lay on the ground.

'Come on,' he said.

She groaned. 'Do we have to?'

' 'Fraid so.' Pitt helped her up.

'Are the Hennesseys coming after us?' Thora was too exhausted to even sound scared.

'No, don't worry. Belle is still at the bottom of the slope—' Pitt grinned. Even from here he could see anger in every line of her body. She must be spitting feathers at having been bested by Thora. 'Bobby-Jo and Leapman are climbing the hill but they're obviously just going after Burchell's body. Their horses are below with Belle.'

'Thank God.'

'I doubt they'll even attempt to follow us now and if they do we'll have too good a headstart for them to catch up. And I can take the time to hide our tracks properly. But it's getting dark and we've a way to go. We must get on.'

'Do you know where we are?'

'Not exactly,' Pitt admitted. 'But if we head north we should be going in the right direction. We'll keep to the high country for a while and then head back down towards the hills. We'll reach the farm sooner or later.' He thought he probably sounded more sure of himself than he really was.

He hoisted Thora up into the saddle. She slumped forward over the pommel, too tired to do anything more than cling on and hope she didn't fall asleep and fall off. Pitt caught hold of the reins of her horse so he could lead it.

Before they had gone very far night closed in and it quickly became pitch dark and freezing cold.

'What are we going to do?' Thora asked, trying hard to stop her teeth from chattering.

'We might have to stop and make camp somewhere,' Pitt said, even though he didn't want to. Although he could make and start a fire he had no means of even boiling up some coffee let alone making them anything to eat. And he feared the Hennesseys might see the fire and work out it was them and where they were. 'But we'll go on a little while yet.' He ignored Thora's moan.

He was thinking of giving up when at last he thought he glimpsed a faint light in the distance. A short while later they emerged into a clearing and across the way he saw a low building. Lamplight spilled out from cracks in the window shutters, revealing a barn and small corral, where a horse and a milk cow grazed, while wood was stacked against the side of the house. This must be the Walkers' farm. They'd made it.

'We're there,' he said, voice cracking in relief. He reached across to shake Thora who by now was almost asleep and brought their horses to a halt.

'Are we safe?'

'Yeah.' Pitt called out, 'Hey, you there, in the house.'

A few seconds later the door opened and a man and woman came out. The woman was holding an oil lamp and the man a shotgun, which he looked quite capable of using.

'Who is it?'

'We've come from Marshal Kirkpatrick in Felicidad. We need your help.'

'Come on ahead. Slowly.' The man raised his gun, obviously about to take no chances. 'You're out late. And,' he added suspiciously as they rode into the lamplight, 'in a terrible mess.'

Pitt wondered what a picture they must make. Both covered from head to foot in mud. Clothes torn. His hat lost somewhere. Hands and faces scratched and bruised. He wouldn't blame Fred Walker for turning them away or shooting them.

'We had a run-in with the Hennesseys.'

The Walkers exchanged glances.

'Please help us,' Thora said, scared the couple were going to go back inside and shut the door. I won't cry, she told herself, I won't be such a ninny. I won't . . . she burst into tears.

'Oh, my dear,' Mrs Walker said and came forward to help Thora off her horse. 'What on earth has happened to you? There, there don't cry. It'll be all right. Fred, you see to the horses, while I look after these two.'

'All right,' Walker said then turning to Pitt added, 'But no trouble understand?'

'Fred, look at them! They're in no state to cause trouble!'

Wearily Pitt slid out of the saddle and followed Mrs Walker as she helped Thora into the house. What he needed, he decided, was some warmth, something to eat and first of all a good wash. Get rid of the mud clinging to his hands and in his hair.

It was much too late to go back to Felicidad now, even if he could find the energy to try and he hoped Kirkpatrick wouldn't be so worried he'd leave the jailhouse to come looking for them.

He had a feeling the Hennesseys would quickly hatch some other plan to free their father and Kirkpatrick's place was in Felicidad so he could defeat them. In fact, Pitt decided he wanted to be back in time to help Kirkpatrick do just that. Meanwhile there was nothing he could do until morning.

CHAPTER NINETEEN

Pitt left the Walkers' farm almost as soon as dawn streaked the Eastern sky. The Walkers were already up and about: Fred to care for the animals and Ruth to cook breakfast, making Pitt think yet again how hard life on a farm was. Thora was still asleep, worn out by her ordeal.

'Don't worry,' Walker said as Pitt mounted his horse. 'We'll look after her.'

'I doubt it'll be for long. The situation will be sorted out soon, one way or the other.'

Walker nodded sombrely.

By the time Pitt reached Felicidad it was still early, not many people about, the stores not yet open. He left his tired horse at the stables to be cared for and walked through the almost empty streets to the jail-house. As he neared it, the door opened and Kirkpatrick rushed out.

'Pitt, what's happened? How's Thora? Is she all right? I expected you back yesterday.'

Pitt held up a hand. 'Thora's fine. She's at the farm.'

'Thank God!' Kirkpatrick let out the breath he'd

been holding. 'How did you get on? Did the Hennesseys follow you?'

'Yeah but we managed to give them the slip. Miss Dowling was very brave. She got the better of Belle.' That made Kirkpatrick smile. 'And Charley Burchell is either dead or badly wounded.'

He followed the marshal into his office where Kirkpatrick poured out freshly made coffee. Sitting down, he quickly related his story and then, just as quickly, Kirkpatrick told him about shooting Jake Carney.

'And Lizzie's OK, is she?'

'According to Mrs Barron, she will be. I'm sorry, Pitt, I should have taken more notice of your warning me that Lizzie might be in danger.'

'And you don't expect any problem over Carney?'

'No. Everyone I've spoken to is relieved Carney is dead. All except Old Man Hennessey of course. They were pals.' Kirkpatrick smiled.

'I'll have to visit Lizzie later on today.'

'She'd like that.' Kirkpatrick's voice turned serious. 'Bobby-Jo won't be able to follow your trail to the farm, will he?'

'I'm sure not. With them giving up the chase I had time to wipe out our tracks before it got too dark. And then we spent some while riding through the stream and when we came out it was amongst some rocks where our tracks will be hard to find.'

Kirkpatrick nodded in satisfaction.

'Anyway I doubt whether they'll bother. I think they'll concentrate on trying to get their pa out of jail.'

'Me too. They'll probably try to take me by surprise. What are you going to do now?'

'I'd better go on down to The Silver Dollar, find out if I've still got a job there.'

'OK. And, Pitt, thanks.'

It was a long, hot day. Kirkpatrick spent most of it walking round the town, reassuring the nervous that he had the situation under control and that the Hennesseys wouldn't do anything he couldn't handle. Vaughan stayed in the jailhouse, along with a couple of younger townsmen who were disappointed in their hopes of getting involved in a shoot-out with Bobby-Jo and Leapman.

Lizzie came to for a short while to find Pitt sitting by her bedside. She smiled before slipping back into sleep. The cuts and weals on her body made Pitt wish he'd been the one to shoot Carney.

And Bobby-Jo, Belle and Leapman sat in a grove of cottonwoods just outside of Felicidad, waiting for night to fall.

That evening Kirkpatrick sent the townsmen home and then told Dave Vaughan to get something to eat.

'Afterwards you'd better patrol the town while I wait here.' He looked at his deputy. 'I'm afraid it's going to be another long night and it'll be a long few days unless and until Bobby-Jo tries to free his pa.'

Vaughan shrugged. 'It goes with the job.'

'And be careful.'

'You too.'

Kirkpatrick locked and barred the jailhouse door behind Vaughan. He sat at the desk, rifle close at hand, knowing he had another lonely night to get through. His one consolation was that Thora was out of danger.

It was just after midnight that Bobby-Jo, Belle and Leapman rode into Felicidad. They had a spare horse with them for Old Man Hennessey to ride when they rescued him. They came to a halt near to the livery stable.

They had decided to leave their horses there and approach the jail on foot, because anyone looking out of a window was more likely to see three riders than people slipping by in the shadows. Once the shooting started they were sure there would be enough confusion for them to get back to the horses before anyone realized what was going on.

'You both know what to do, don't you?' Belle had decided to take charge and it was she who had decided what they were going to do. 'We'll use the alleys to reach the jail.'

'Yeah, don't worry,' Leapman said. He was angry because neither he nor Bobby-Jo liked taking orders from Belle. He looked round at the livery stable.

'What's the matter?' Bobby-Jo asked.

'I thought I heard something.'

Bobby-Jo followed his gaze. 'There's no one there. You're imagining things. Let's go.'

But Leapman was right. Vaughan was taking a rest in the stables. He'd seen them ride up. Knew they planned trouble. Now he hitched up his gunbelt and took off for the jailhouse at a run, hoping he got there before they did.

Kirkpatrick was dozing when Vaughan banged on the door. 'Marshal! Marshal, open up!'

Kirkpatrick jerked awake. Reaching over, he quickly doused the oil lamp and grabbing up the rifle, moved to the door. He opened it and Vaughan fell inside.

'They're coming!' the man said breathlessly. 'They're right behind me.'

At the same time shots opened up from the opposite side of the road.

Kirkpatrick caught hold of Vaughan's arm and propelled him into the office. 'Get in the cells, make sure Hennessey stays put.'

Even as Vaughan hurried to do what he was told, Hennessey called out, 'Now you get yours, Marshal! My kids are here!'

'Shut up,' Kirkpatrick muttered under his breath and began to return the gunfire from across the way.

At the rear Belle climbed over the wall and ran across the small exercise yard to the cell windows.

'Pa! Pa, where are you?'

'In here, where else?' Hennessey called back. ' 'Bout time you showed up, girl.'

'We're getting you out.'

'You can't get in from the back, the door's too strong,' Hennessey's voice was angry and impatient. 'Go on round to the front, help your brother. And hurry it up.'

'Here's a gun, Pa.' And Belle threw a pistol up to the window. Somehow it slid through the bars and landed on the floor of the cell.

Even as Hennessey was reaching for it, Vaughan yelled at him, 'Get away from it. Get away!' He pointed his gun at the man. 'I'll shoot you.' With a slightly shaky hand he unlocked the cell door.

Hennessey debated on whether or not he could reach the gun before Vaughan could fire. But the odds were against him and while he considered Vaughan fat and stupid, he didn't like the gleam in the deputy's eyes. Then the moment was lost and furious with himself for not taking the chance he stepped away and raised his hands.

Vaughan kicked the gun out of the cell and slammed the door shut.

'My boy'll kill you,' Hennessey yelled at him. 'And I'll watch while he does it. You can't win agin us Hennesseys.'

Down in The Silver Dollar, Pitt was in the middle of the first profitable poker-game he'd played since coming to Felicidad. He'd already won several hands and now he held a full house, of three kings and two fives – surely a winning hand – with a pile of money bet on the table in front of him. Then the shooting started.

'Oh hell!' he said. Although it meant losing money he didn't hesitate. Much to the surprise of the other players he threw the cards down, said, 'I'm out,' and ran for the door.

'Get him!' Leapman yelled.

Bobby-Jo sprang from his hiding place and raced across the street towards the jailhouse, firing as he came.

Kirkpatrick was pushing shut the door when a bullet struck his shoulder, sending him tumbling backwards. Bobby-Jo yelled in triumph and rushed him. From his position on the floor Kirkpatrick raised his rifle and fired at point-blank range. The bullet took Bobby-Jo in the neck. With a surprised look on his face he skittered back across the sidewalk and hit against the hitching rail. It shattered beneath him and he fell through the air, landing on the ground with a heavy thump.

Belle ran round the side of the building just as her brother died. 'Bobby-Jo!'

Leapman also got to his feet. 'Kirkpatrick's down. Get him, Belle!' He started across the street.

He didn't see Pitt coming towards the jailhouse from the opposite direction. Pitt raised the gun he already held and still at a run sent several bullets towards Leapman. One of the slugs struck the foreman at the same moment as he shot at Kirkpatrick. Leapman jerked in fright and agony and his bullet missed the marshal and hit Belle instead.

Belle screamed and came to a shuddering halt. She collapsed near to her brother's body.

Pitt shot Leapman and the man went down.

Several townsmen, led by Mr Toombs, came running up in support.

Pitt hurried over to Kirkpatrick. 'You hit?'

'It's my shoulder,' Kirkpatrick said, struggling to his feet and clutching at his arm. 'Dave, everything all right in there?'

'Yeah.'

'Stay where you are then.'

Together with Pitt, Kirkpatrick left his office and went up to Belle. He crouched down by her.

The girl's front was covered in red, sticky blood and each breath she took was shallow and made with a dreadful effort. Her eyes opened and she looked at the two men but it was doubtful she recognized them.

'Am I dying?' she gasped.

'I'm afraid so, Belle,' Kirkpatrick said. 'I'm sorry.'

'Me too.' She tried to smile, making her hard face turn softer and younger. 'Weren't your fault. It's being a Hennessey. Tell, Pa . . .' Belle's breath caught in her throat and fright flared in her eyes. Then her head dropped back and she was gone.

Kirkpatrick sighed, closed her eyes and stood up. 'Wonder what she wanted her pa to know?'

Pitt shrugged.

'Bobby-Jo and Leapman are both dead,' Toombs said as he came up to them. 'What about Belle?'

'Yes, she's dead too. It was an accident. Leapman's bullet hit her instead of me.'

'These things happen,' Pitt said. 'She knew the chances she was taking.'

'I suppose so.'

'Ralph, the Hennesseys were bent on freeing their pa. They'd've killed you and anyone else who got in their way. And that includes Thora.'

'He's right,' Toombs added.

'If you want to continue as Felicidad's marshal you'll have to put Belle's death out of your mind. That is if you do want to go on?'

Aware of everyone looking at him anxiously,

Kirkpatrick thought about that for a while.

'Yeah I do.'

'Good.'

'Well, one thing is for sure,' Pitt said. 'The days of the Hennesseys terrorizing the town are over.'

Kirkpatrick nodded. 'And Old Man Hennessey is still in jail waiting his trial. In fact, he's probably wondering why he is still locked up.' He gave a little smile. 'I'd better go and tell him the bad news. And tell him his son and daughter are dead. Somehow I don't think he'll be that upset about them. His main concern will be himself.'

'Perhaps Belle wanted to tell him to go to hell,' Pitt said.

'I'd like to think so.'

CHAPTER TWENTY

Thora insisted on helping the Walkers in return for letting her stay at the farmhouse. But after she'd finished whatever they needed doing, she spent the rest of the time on the porch staring down the trail that led towards Felicidad.

How long would she have to wait? Perhaps until Judge Corbett arrived and she was needed to testify against Hennessey. How long would that be? A week at least. Perhaps longer. She'd never be able to stand not knowing what was happening for all that time. Waiting she decided was even worse than being chased across the hills, covered with mud and being shot at.

Luckily for her peace of mind, she didn't have to wait that long.

It was late morning of her second day on the farm when she spotted two horsemen coming up the hillside. Immediately Fred Walker was beside her, shotgun cradled in his arms, ready to send her inside.

'No,' she told him. 'It's not the Hennesseys. It's Mr Pitt, I recognize his horse.'

What was he doing here? Was anything wrong?

And who was the second rider? They were too far away, riding in and out of the trees, for her to tell. Oh, please, please, let it be Ralph. Her heart missed several beats. Supposing Mr Pitt was coming to tell her that something had happened to Ralph. Oh, please, please, let Ralph be all right.

Then she squealed in delight. The second rider had paused to wave at her. It was Ralph! He was here! His arm was in a sling! Oh no, he'd been hurt. Surely not badly or he wouldn't have been able to ride all the way out here!

Aware of the Walkers by her side, smiling at her, she jumped down from the porch and ran towards him. At the same time Kirkpatrick got off his horse.

They met in the middle of the yard.

'It's all right, sweetheart,' Kirkpatrick said, holding her as if he never intended to let her go. 'It's all over. Me and Pitt are here to take you home.'

Home!

'Yes, Ralph, please.'